DETECTIVE BEN

Ben the tramp, the awkward Cockney with no home and no surname, turns detective again – and runs straight into trouble.

Son of novelist Benjamin Farjeon, and brother to children's author Eleanor, playwright Herbert and composer Harry, Joseph Jefferson Farjeon (1883–1955) began work as an actor and freelance journalist before inevitably turning his own hand to writing fiction. Described by the *Sunday Times* as 'a master of the art of blending horrors with humour', Farjeon was a prolific author of mystery novels, with more than 60 books published between 1924 and 1955. His first play, *No. 17*, was produced at the New Theatre in 1925, when the actor Leon M. Lion 'made all London laugh' as Ben the tramp, an unorthodox amateur detective who became the most enduring of all Farjeon's creations. Rewritten as a novel in 1926 and filmed by Alfred Hitchcock six years later, with Mr Lion reprising his role, *No.17*'s success led to seven further books featuring the warm-hearted but danger-prone Ben: 'Ben is not merely a character but a parable—a mixture of Trimalchio and the Old Kent Road, a notable coward, a notable hero, above all a supreme humourist' (Seton Dearden, *Time and Tide*). Although he had become largely forgotten over the 60 years since his death, J. Jefferson Farjeon's reputation made an impressive resurgence in 2014 when his 1937 Crime Club book *Mystery in White* was reprinted by the British Library, returning him to the bestseller lists and resulting in readers wanting to know more about this enigmatic author from the Golden Age of detective fiction.

Also in this series

J. JEFFERSON FARJEON

Detective Ben

COLLINS
CRIME
CLUB

COLLINS CRIME CLUB
An imprint of HarperCollins*Publishers*
1 London Bridge Street
London SE1 9GF
www.harpercollins.co.uk

This paperback edition 2016

First published in Great Britain for The Crime Club Ltd
by W. Collins Sons & Co. Ltd 1936

A catalogue record for this book is
available from the British Library

ISBN 978-0-00-815600-8

Set in Sabon by Palimpsest Book Production Limited, Falkirk, Stirlingshire

Printed by Clays Ltd, St Ives plc

MIX
Paper from
responsible sources
FSC
www.fsc.org
FSC C007454

Contents

1

Happenings on a Bridge

'I wouldn't mate, if I was you,' said Ben. 'It looks narsty!'

Thus, on a bridge at night, spoke one ragged man to another. Beneath them oozed dark water wending its inscrutable way towards the sea. Above them were the stars.

'Mindjer, I ain't sayin' that life's plumpunnin',' continued Ben, since his observation elicited no response. 'If yer was to arsk me wot it was orl abart, I couldn't tell yer, that's a fack. Yer born without so much as by yer leave, and then they chucks yer this way and that till yer fair giddy. But—well, we gotter 'ang on—that's right, ain't it? England expecks every man to 'ang on, Gawd knows why, but yer can't git away from it. 'Ang on!' He paused to peer downwards at the inky river. 'Any'ow, if I ever does pop meself orf, I'd sooner do it with a bang than a gurgle!'

He removed his eyes from the inky river. It wasn't a pleasant sight. A moment later he was looking at another unpleasant sight. A small object gleamed up from the

1

pavement by the stone parapet, and stooping to pick it up he discovered that it was a pin on which was mounted a miniature skull.

'Well, I'm blowed!' he muttered. 'Do yer belong to one o' them Suissicide Clubs?'

He held the hideous little decoration out to his ragged companion. Then he found himself staring at the most unpleasant sight of all. The dejected attitude in which his companion was leaning over the parapet was not that of a man contemplating death, but of a man already dead!

Ben had seen plenty of dead men in his time. It seemed to him that as soon as a person died, Fate rang for him to come and view the body. 'Lumme, I've stopped noticin' 'em!' he had once boasted. But the boast had been bravado. He always noticed them, and they always affected his spine. This one affected his legs, as well, and before he knew it he was twenty yards away. Run first and think afterwards. That was his Napoleonic motto.

In the distance chimed a clock. The metallic notes hung slow and heavy on the air. One—two. Then from the direction of the chiming came another sound. The sound of an approaching car.

'If yer runs, they'll 'ave yer for it,' Ben told himself with a gulp. 'Stay where yer are and look 'appy.'

The only thing he had to be happy about was the substantial shadow in which he stood.

The approaching car drew closer. It also grew larger. Watching it from his shadowy sanctuary as it sped on to the bridge, Ben was impressed by the fact that it was not an ordinary car. That, perhaps, was not surprising, since nothing at this moment was ordinary. Ben's mood was not ordinary. The bridge was not ordinary; it had become distorted into a grotesque, unnatural travesty of itself, painted with the sinister insecurity of nightmare colours. The little pin with its miniature skull was not ordinary. The ragged figure leaning limply against the parapet twenty yards away was not ordinary . . .

Nor was the behaviour of the car when it reached the ragged figure.

The car stopped suddenly. Why did it remind one of hospitals? Five men leapt out, violently invading the peace that had reigned uncannily a few moments before. Two of the men were policemen. Two of the others had an official atmosphere. The fifth had no official atmosphere. He wore an ordinary lounge suit and a squash felt hat and he stood a little apart, watching and smoking, while the others proceeded swiftly and smoothly with their business.

A stretcher appeared from the interior of the car. The ragged fellow into whose deaf ear Ben had tried to pass a little human comfort—posthumous comfort that only God had heard—was lifted on to the stretcher and carried into the car. Now there only remained his memory, and already the inevitable process of wiping out had begun. Ben stared at the portion of parapet against which the fellow had been leaning. Had he ever really been there? How many people would lean against the very same spot tomorrow, ignorant of their contact with tragedy?

Now the five men were talking. Their voices made a low, lugubrious buzz. Ben thought of bees. What happened when bees died? Did one bee report it, and others come along and take it out of the hive? It was a nuisance—Ben's mind working like that! Jumping about just when he wanted to keep it steady. Perhaps it would have kept steadier on three good meals a day . . . Hallo! The car was filling up again.

It was turning. In another moment the car, like the ragged fellow, would only be a memory, to recede unexplained into oblivion while life moved sluggishly on.

But Ben was wrong. This car would not recede into oblivion. It would remain for ever in his memory, and the thread that held him to it now, even after it had vanished from the bridge, was the man in the squash felt hat. He had stayed behind, having been temporarily obscured by the car while the others had re-entered it, and the steady glow of his cigarette made a pin-point in the dimness.

Ben found himself watching the glow. In a queer way it held him rooted, like a snake's magnetic eye. Would it never move, and release him? If he moved first, out of the shadow, he would be spotted without a doubt.

'Well, I ain't done nothink!' his thoughts suddenly rebelled. 'I'm goin'!'

These unpleasant seconds were getting on his nerves. But before he could act upon his decision a voice called to him quietly across the road.

'Stay where you are, or get a bullet!'

'That's done it!' reflected Ben miserably. 'Quick—think of a story!'

His mind refused to respond, and when the man in the squash felt hat, a revolver now added to his visible equipment, had traversed the intervening twenty yards, Ben had nothing between him and the law but the naked truth. And, after all, what was wrong with the truth?

'Who are you?' asked the man.

'Bloke,' replied Ben.

'What sort of a bloke?'

''Ollywood star.'

You might as well die game. Life couldn't be an utter

failure if you made your last word a joke. It was a pity, though, that the man with the revolver didn't smile at the joke.

'Let's try again,' said the man. He had patience, anyway. 'What are you doing here?'

'Eh?'

'What are you doing here?'

'Nothink.'

'Ever heard of the truth?'

'Well, wotjer want me to say?' demanded Ben. 'Pickin' 'ops?'

'I've no doubt you're quite good at hopping,' remarked the man, dryly, 'but two o'clock in the morning is rather late to be hopping about, isn't it?'

'It's early fer me.'

'Never go to bed?'

'Yus. On'y they ain't turned dahn the sheets yet at The Ritz.'

This time the man did smile. Ben smiled back, trying to consolidate the happier atmosphere. Funny, what a smile did! Couple of blokes meet, all glum. One of 'em smiles. Blinkin' sun comes out!

'Been here long?' the man inquired next.

'Depends wot yer call long,' answered Ben cautiously. 'Long fer a toothache, but not fer a nap.'

'An hour?'

'Lumme, no!'

'Five minutes?'

Now for it! Ben took a deep breath and trusted to luck. 'Abart that,' he replied. 'Or p'r'aps six.'

'Six,' repeated the man, thoughtfully. 'Not longer?' Ben shook his head. 'But six was long enough for you to see something interesting?'

'Yer mean—the deader?'

'Yes. The deader?'

'That's right. I see 'im.'

'Well?'

'Well wot? I didn't dead 'im.'

'I know you didn't.'

'Go on!'

'You couldn't have.'

'That's right, sir. I didn't of. But 'ow did you know? Every time anythink 'appens this side o' China, it's always Ben wot's done it!'

'Ben?'

'That's me. 'Aven't yer never bought me on a postcard?'

The man in the squash felt hat stared at Ben rather hard. Solemnly Ben stared back. Then the man said:

'I'll tell you how I know you didn't kill that fellow, Ben. I killed him myself.'

Ben opened his mouth and gaped at this self-described murderer. Lumme, he didn't look that sort! But, of course, he had a revolver. Ben closed his mouth to swallow, then whispered hoarsely:

'Coppers didn't know, eh?'

'Oh, yes, they knew,' responded the man. 'The chap was a wrong 'un.'

'Well, I'm jiggered!' murmured Ben. 'And I thort 'e was jest a poor bloke like me!'

The man glanced at him sharply.

'Oh—you knew something about him, then?'

'Eh?'

'What made you think he was just a poor bloke like you?'

'Oh! Well—I come upon 'im, see? And findin' 'im leanin' there—well, orl crumpled like, I felt sorry fer 'im—you

know, it bein' late and orl that—and as I thort 'e was goin'
to commit suissicide I spoke to 'im—'

'You *spoke* to him?'

'I'm tellin' yer. I didn't know 'e was dead. I gener'ly seen
'em stiff. But, corse, that's arter.'

'Arter?'

'Yus. Limp fust, stiff arter. "Doncher go chuckin' yerself
over," I ses to 'im. "Stick it aht, mate," I ses. That's right,
ain't it? And then I looks at 'im a bit closer like—'cos 'e
didn't say nothink, see?—and, Gawd, 'e looks back at me
from the nex' Kingdom, if yer git me. It was—narsty.'

'I'm sure it must have been,' replied the man, with a
note of sympathy. 'And then what did you do?'

'I arsk yer!' answered Ben.

'No, I'm asking you!'

'Eh? Oh! Well, I come over 'ere.'

'Why?'

''Cos 'e was over there.'

'It sounds a good reason.'

'You bet it was a good reason. If yer lookin' for a 'ero,
guv'nor, it ain't no good lookin' at me! And arter that, the
police car comes along, and now you've got the lot.'

'No, there's one more thing,' said the man, lowering his
eyes from Ben's face.

'Wot?' asked Ben.

'The thing you've got in your hand,' responded the man.
'How did you get hold of *that*?'

Now Ben lowered his own eyes, also.

'Lumme, 'ave I still got it?' he muttered. Clutched in
his fingers was the ugly little skullpin. 'Well, it ain't *my*
pickcher!'

'Where did you find it?'

'On the ground. By the dead bloke. I was jest 'andin' it back to 'im when I fahnd out—'

He stopped short and shivered, recalling the unsavoury moment.

'When you found out that he was past needing it?' queried the man.

'That's it, guv'nor.'

'But how did you know it was his?'

'I didn't know. Come ter that, I don't know. But yer puts two and two tergether, doncher, so I jest thort it might be, seein' as 'ow it was next to 'is boot, and thinkin', don't fergit, that 'e belonged to one o' them Suissicide Clubs.'

The man nodded, and regarded the pin meditatively.

'Yes, it was his,' he said.

'Then wotcher arskin' me for?' demanded Ben.

'I didn't ask you if it was his, I asked you how you knew it was his. It was in his coat. I expect it must have dropped out.'

'Well, I don't want it in *my* coat!' declared Ben emphatically. 'Yer can 'ave it fer a birthday present.'

But the man did not take the offering. Instead he continued to regard it for a few seconds, and then raised his eyes again to Ben's face.

'In *your* coat,' he murmured. 'That's an idea!'

'Oh! Well, I ain't 'avin' the idea!' retorted Ben. 'And if yer've finished with me, can I go?'

The man made no answer. He seemed to be thinking hard. Suddenly it occurred to Ben that perhaps *he* was entitled to ask a question.

'Wotcher kill 'im for, guv'nor?' he inquired.

'It was self-defence,' said the man.

'Ah—'e went fer yer?'

8

'That's it.'

'Why?'

'Let's say—a guilty conscience. I told you he was a wrong 'un.'

'Yus. Well, if 'e went fer yer, they can't 'ang yer.'

'Thanks for the consolation. But if they'd wanted to hang me, would those bobbies have left me behind?'

'So they wouldn't!'

'Getting wise?'

'Yer mean, yer a 'tec?'

The man nodded. 'But even detectives make mistakes sometimes—'

'Go on!'

'—and I showed myself a bit too soon. Don't ask any more questions for the moment. Just stand by. I'm thinking. Maybe—you can help me.'

''Ow luvverly!' murmured Ben.

A new sense of discomfort began to enter into him. He was no longer afraid of this man. He was no longer threatened by either a revolver or the gallows. But he was threatened by something else—something that lurked in the grinning little skull he was holding, and the detective's last words, and the depressingly likeable quality of the detective's eyes. He was the sort of man you might easily make a silly fool of yourself for. Yes, you wanted to be careful of him, or you'd promise yourself into a pack of trouble!

'Got somethink to tell yer, guv'nor,' said Ben.

'What?' asked the detective.

'I'm a mug. I ain't no good at 'elpin'.'

'I'm not so sure.'

'Well, see, I knows meself better. The on'y thing I'm really good at's runnin' away.'

'Many a useful man begins by running away.'

'Yus, but I've never stopped.'

'You're stopping now.'

'Eh?'

'Prove your words. I'm not keeping you. Run away. Pop off!'

'Lumme, 'e's doin' me!' thought Ben, wretchedly. 'I toljer 'e would.'

'You see, I know you better than you know yourself,' continued the detective, after a pause. 'I'm quite sure you know how to run away—'

'I'll die runnin'!'

'—but if there's any solid reason, you stand firm. You used one of my favourite expressions just now. "Stick it out." Well, suppose I told you that, if you stick *this* out, you may bring off something that will make all the folk in Scotland Yard touch their hats to you every time you pass—'

'Go on!'

'—and that might bring you in, say, a fifty pound note at the end?'

''Ere, 'old me!' gasped Ben.

The detective laughed softly. 'Listen—I'm going to tell you a little story,' he said.

'I'll bet it's 'orrible!'

'But you'd like to hear it?'

'No. Go on.'

'The fellow you spoke to and who has just been taken away had an appointment to meet somebody on this bridge between two and half-past. He was going to be identified by his rags and that skull-pin in your hand. I don't know who the somebody is, but I do know that if I can track

10

him to his source—that's my present job—I'm on to a big thing.'

'Yus, but—'

'Wait till I've finished. What I'm going to propose to you is this. The somebody hasn't turned up yet. Will you wait on this bridge, with that ugly brute of a pin in your coat, at the spot where you spoke to the late lamented, till half-past two—'

'Late 'oo?'

'The chap who's dead. Nothing may happen. In that case the fee will have to be reduced, but you'll still be on to a fiver for the easiest job you've ever had. But something *may* happen. The somebody *may* turn up, and be duped by your rags and your pin. In that case—Ben—if you play your cards cleverly and "stick it out," eh?—the somebody may cart you back to the very source I'm looking for, and you will earn your couple of ponies.'

Ben wiped his forehead.

'I admit it won't be pleasant. But there will be glory and cash at the end of it—and, of course, I'll be following you and looking after you—with *this*—!'

He raised his revolver again and, with grim and unappreciated humour, directed it towards Ben. Ben ducked involuntarily. An instant later the detective dropped to the ground, a crumpled heap.

Ben stared, stunned. 'Wot's 'appened to me?' he wondered. The thing had been too swift and silent and unbelievable to have occurred outside a suddenly distorted brain. His mind ceased to function. Then he experienced a sensation as though he were coming out of gas. Truth developed out of numbness, and for several seconds he saw nothing, and thought of nothing, but the helpless, limp form of a young

11

man whose eager voice still echoed in his ears, and whose friendly eyes had conveyed him out of terror into human warmth . . . He looked up to find other eyes upon him. The eyes of a beautiful woman in a dark, close-fitting coat.

She was standing beside a closed car. Had the car slipped up from the ground? He had not heard its approach. It had come as silently as the bullet. Or perhaps emotion had throbbed too insistently in his ears . . .

'Quick!' ordered the beautiful woman. 'There's not a moment!'

The door of the car was open. Ben looked at it; then at her; and then once more at the motionless heap on the ground.

'Dead?' said Ben thickly.

'Quite,' answered the woman. Her voice was low and rich, but as pitiless as cold steel.

'Are you coming?'

Ben raised his face from death to life. Even in this dimness the woman's eyes were dazzling. Ben's heart turned black.

He nodded.

'That's right, miss,' he murmured. 'I'm comin'.'

2

The Dark Journey

The blackness in Ben's heart was reflected in the car. The blinds were drawn, and as the car shot forward he found himself travelling in a darkness that seemed to creep right up to him and touch him.

By his side was the beautiful woman. Even in this enveloping darkness that affected both sight and soul he remained conscious of her beauty, just as he had been conscious of it while staring at death. It brushed his ragged sleeve as the car swung abruptly round a corner. It whispered to him through the fragrance of scent. It electrified the black atmosphere. Ben was not impervious to beauty, and he could stare with incoherent appreciation at a sunset, or watch little children dancing to a piano-organ, or pause, futilely desirous, at the photograph of a naughty chorus girl wrapped round a pound of cheese. But he hardened himself against the beauty he was now encountering, for it presided in enemy territory.

Ahead of him, driving, was another figure. A big, smudgy figure in a large overcoat. There was no beauty in this dim outline. It was sinister and forbidding, and reminded Ben of Carnera. He found himself wondering how long, if it came to a fight, he would be able to stand up against that massive frame. He worked it out at five seconds less six.

But the big figure in the large overcoat had another kind of tussle on at the moment. Emerging suddenly from his dazed thoughts, Ben became conscious of it when the car took another violent curve that brought the woman's shoulder hard against his own. He heard a shout. The car swerved. He heard a shot. The car accelerated dizzily. Another corner. Straight again. Another corner. Straight again. *Plop! Ting!* Two little holes. One in the small window in the back of the car, one in the windscreen. A straight line between the two holes separated, and cleared by three inches, two heads.

'All right, Fred?' inquired the owner of one of the heads, coolly; while the owner of the other head thought, less coolly, 'Lumme!'

The big figure in the large overcoat nodded. The car flew on.

'And you?' asked the woman, turning to Ben.

It was the first time she had addressed Ben since they had entered the car. 'Now wot I've gotter do,' reflected Ben, 'is to pertend it ain't nothink, like 'er!' Aloud he responded, with elaborate carelessness:

'Corse! 'Oo minds a little thing like that?'

She smiled. He could not see the smile, but he felt it. It came to you, like her scent.

'Item, courage,' were her next words. 'Well, I'm glad you've got that, for you'll need it.'

''Ooray,' thought Ben.

14

'But, after all,' she went on, 'one expects courage from those who have been awarded the D.S.O.'

''Oo's that?' jerked Ben.

'Distinguished Skull Order.' She touched his gruesome pin with a slender finger. 'You must tell me one day what you got it for. I expect you've a nice little selection of bedtime stories. But have you ever been shot at twice in five minutes before? You have to thank our driver for saving you the first time.'

'Eh? When was the fust time?' blinked Ben.

He couldn't remember it, and the notion that he was under any obligation to the driver was not one that went to his heart. When had the ugly brute saved him?

'Don't play poker-face with me!' retorted the woman. 'You know as well as I do! . . . Oh, but of course—I see what you mean. The detective didn't actually shoot at you—he was merely going to. Well, Fred was a fool to interfere. If you'd got in a mess, it was your affair to get out of it. However he lost his head, so I hope you'll prove worth the risk he took by not losing yours!'

Ben's mind swung back to the instant just before the detective had fallen. The detective had raised his revolver. The driver of the approaching car—this hulking brute a couple of feet ahead—had seen and misinterpreted the action. He had fired. The detective had dropped. And, for this, Ben had to thank him!

'One day I'll thank 'im in a way 'e won't fergit!' decided Ben.

Meanwhile, he must keep cool, and organise the few wits he possessed. He would have to display a few of those wits, to justify membership of the Distinguished Skull Order!

'Ah—then it wasn't *you* wot fired the gun?' he murmured. 'It wasn't you wot killed 'im?'

'I never lose my head,' answered the woman, with a contemptuous glance towards the driver's back.

'I didn't 'ear no bang,' said Ben.

'There wasn't any bang,' replied the woman.

'Oh—one o' them things,' nodded Ben. 'That's the kind wot I uses. Orl bite and no bark!'

The driver shifted impatiently in his seat.

'Do you suppose *you* could bark a little less?' he growled. 'We aren't out of the wood yet!'

'Keep your nerve, Fred,' observed the woman calmly. 'We're keeping ours. I rather like our new recruit's Oxford accent.'

Lumme, she was cool! Ben had to concede her that. But so were snakes. They could stay still for an hour. And then—*bing*!

A minute later, while a police whistle sounded faintly in the distance, the car turned up a by-street and stopped. The woman opened the door and leapt out with the speed of a cat. Ben followed obediently. The driver remained in his seat.

'Be with you in five minutes,' the driver muttered.

The whistle sounded again, not quite so distantly.

'No, you won't, Fred,' said the woman. 'Five hours, at least!'

'Oh! What's the idea?'

'That you use the wits God is supposed to have given you. If you can't shake off the police, you're no good to me.'

'Well, haven't I—?'

She held up a hand. The whistle sounded a third time, closer still.

'Listen, and don't argue! That car's been marked, and *you're* wanted for murder. Both unhealthy. I'm not recognising you till you've left the car in a ditch forty miles away. Have you got that?'

'Do I leave myself in the ditch with the car?'

'That's a question of personal choice.'

'Suppose I'm caught?'

'Then I certainly won't recognise you. But it's not your habit to be caught.'

'All right—suppose I'm not caught?'

'You'll change your appearance.'

'And then?'

'Then you can come home to mother, darling, and she'll give you a—'

'What?'

'A nice new pinafore.'

She smiled, and suddenly the driver grinned. 'She can twist 'im rahnd 'er finger!' decided Ben. 'On'y got to show 'er teeth!'

He wondered what would happen if he gave the sudden shout that was bursting for expression inside him. Would the woman still remain cool and collected? More important, would the chauffeur lose his head a second time and add another capital crime to his sheet?

But it was not fear of these things, though undoubtedly he feared them, that urged Ben to restrain his violent impulse. It was the memory of the detective lying on the bridge. Ben was carrying on for the detective. He was in his official shoes—a detective, now, himself! And he meant to remain one until he had done all his predecessor had set out to do—and a little bit more!

The woman raised her head sharply. A car had turned abruptly into the next street at racing speed.

17

'You'll lose your pinafore,' said the woman.

'*Will* I!' retorted the chauffeur.

In a flash he had vanished.

'The cleverest driver and the biggest fool in the kingdom,' murmured the woman.

Ben felt her magnetic fingers on his sleeve. A queer collaboration, those perfect nails upon his threadbare cloth! Guided by the fingers, he moved into the darkness of a doorway. He was used to doorways. He had sheltered in them, pondered in them, shivered in them, dried in them, eaten cheese in them, slept in them, but he had never learned to love them. There was always a haunting ignorance of what lay on the other side. This doorway, for instance. From what was it separating him? People sleeping? People listening? Rats? Emptiness? Dust? . . .

The racing car came whizzing round the corner. Thoughts of the doorway melted into a confusing consciousness of speed and scent in conflict. The speed of the car and the scent of the woman. Movement chasing immobility. Immobility out-witting movement. The scent had never seemed more insistent that at this moment. Inside the car it had seemed natural. Out in a chilly street there was something unreal about it. Like sandwiches after the party's over . . .

Swish! The police-car whizzed by. The metallic hum rose to a shriek, decreased, and faded out into a memory.

'And that's that,' said the woman.

'You fer the brines,' muttered Ben, deeming it the time for a little flattery.

'What about your brains?' she asked.

Ben used them, and touched the little skull that adorned his lapel.

'Would I be wearin' this 'ere skelington if I 'adn't none?' he replied.

'I don't expect you would.'

'Betcher life I wouldn't!'

'What have you done to earn it?'

What had he done? Lumme! What was he supposed to have done? In the absence of any knowledge regarding his back history, he decided to generalise.

'Yer know that bloke wot you called Fred, miss?' he said.

'I've heard of him,' agreed the woman.

'I expeck 'e's done a bit?'

'You've had some evidence of that.'

'Eh? Yus! Well, if yer was to tike orl *'e's* done and if yer was to put it alongside o' wot *I've* done, yer'd lose it!'

'Really?' smiled the woman.

'That's a fack,' answered Ben.

'Then *you* don't mind killing people?'

'Eh?'

'I said, *you* don't mind murder?'

'It's me fav'rit 'obby.'

'Then come inside, and I may show you how to indulge in your hobby,' said the woman. And, producing a Yale key, she inserted it in the door.

3

Questions without Answers

As the key slipped into the lock and turned, Ben rebelled against his own heroism. What was he doing all this for? What would he gain out of it? Why did he not swing round and run, while he still had a chance? Once he was within this house—and the door was already swinging inwards, widening its mouth to receive him—there would be little chance of escape. Apparently he was going in to kill somebody; or, failing that, to be killed himself! Neither alternative brought any comfort to his soul.

Yes, that was what he would do! Turn and run for it. A couple of leaps, then a quick sprawl flat for the bullet—there was bound to be a bullet—then a pancake slide, then up and repeat, and then *bing* round the corner! One, two, three—go!

But he did not go. The power of a live woman or of a dead man held him there, and when the live woman touched his shoulder and the dead man watched to see how he would respond, he walked ahead of her into the yawning black gap, and heard the door close behind him with a soft click.

He had wondered what lay on the other side of the door. Well, now here he was—and no wiser! Blackness lay all around him; a blackness more terrifying, though he could not have explained why, than the blackness inside the car. The space inside the car had been confined. The space here was suffocating.

He heard the woman groping. He decided that conversation would give the best appearance of a courage that was not there.

'Feelin' fer the light?' he asked.

'We don't need a light,' replied the woman.

'Oh, don't we?' murmured Ben. 'Then 'ow do we see?'

'We'll see in a minute,' she answered.

Now she was pressing something. A faint metallic drone responded. It seemed to come from heaven—if heaven still existed. Gradually it descended from the distant elevation, growing more distinct each second. A dim radiance appeared, gleaming through metal slats. 'Corse, it's a lift,' thought Ben.

The lift reached their level and stopped. The drone ceased. A perfect hand reached over Ben's shoulder—the woman was keeping studiously behind him—and pushed the gate aside.

'What are you waiting for?' she asked.

''Oo's waitin'?' retorted Ben.

He stepped in. The woman followed him and closed the gate. She pressed a button. The lift began to ascend, obeying a little finger that had power over the animate as well as the inanimate.

'Which department are we goin' to?' inquired Ben. 'Gimes and toys?'

'You're rather amusing,' answered the woman.

'Yus, reg'ler Charlie Chaplin. I mike the Chimber of 'Orrors larf.'

'Do you make your victims laugh?'

'That's right. Tell 'em a limerick and kill 'em.'

The journey in the lift seemed endless, and the endlessness was accentuated by the fact that there were no glimpses of intermediate floors. The lift travelled up a long, unbroken shaft, giving Ben the sense that they would eventually emerge out of a large chimney.

''Ow much longer?' he asked.

As he put the question the lift stopped. He stared at a blank wall beyond the metal gate.

'Lumme, we've stuck!' he muttered.

'No, we haven't,' said the woman. 'Turn round.'

He turned, and realised for the first time that there was another gate on the other side. It slid open as he stared at it, and so did a polished door. Now he stared into a luxurious little hall, with a soft purple carpet and heavily shaded lights. The rich comfort of the hall gave it a thoroughly unmurderous appearance . . . No, he wasn't so sure. There was something sinister in the very softness of the carpet, something brooding in the stillness . . . Don't be silly! Of course the place was still! You didn't expect to see chairs and tables jumping about, did you?

'Aren't you going to move?' asked the woman.

'That's right,' answered Ben, jerking forward. 'I was jest admirin' of it, like.'

She followed him out, closed the gate, and slid the polished wooden door across. There was now no sign of the lift, for the door resembled the panelled wall on either side. They stood and faced each other in another world.

'Do you approve?' she inquired, with cynical amusement in her eyes.

''Ome from 'ome,' replied Ben.

'That's satisfactory, since it may be your home for some little while. You know, of course, that you'll be staying here till your next journey?'

'Eh?'

'Is your hearing bad?'

'No. It's a 'abit. So there's goin' to be another journey, is there?'

'You didn't suppose you were engaged for a short joy-ride in a car, did you?'

She spoke a little impatiently, but Ben guessed it would be a mistake to appear cowed.

'If that was a joy-ride,' he observed, 'give me a chunk o' misery. When do I start on this other journey?'

'When I tell you.'

'When'll that be?'

'Tomorrow—the next day—next week—next year. You'll know when it happens.'

'Wot—yer means I've gotter sleep 'ere?'

'Of course! I gather already that apparent denseness is a part of your particular method, and I don't say it's a bad idea. I was told you were an unusual man. But you can shed your denseness with me, if you don't mind, and save a lot of time. Now I'll show you your room—and remember this instruction. You are to go into no other.'

'Yus, but I ain't brought my perjamers,' remarked Ben.

She led him across the purple carpet to a passage. The passage was also carpeted, and their feet made no sound as they went along it. They passed two doors, one on each

23

side. Ben strained his ears, but heard nothing behind the doors. No one came out of them.

Were he and the woman alone in the place? The evidence pointed to it.

He risked a leading question.

'Orl the fambily asleep?' he asked.

The question produced no reply. She was depressingly uncommunicative. They reached the end of the passage. Its termination was another door. She pointed to it.

'Go in there,' she ordered, 'and don't come out till you're called.'

'Do I put me boots out?' he inquired.

'Listen!' she answered. 'You've begun well, and I think you will do. There may be times when I will even enjoy your humour. But bear this in mind. You haven't been engaged to play in a comedy.'

Whereupon she opened the door, pushed him in, and then closed the door. An instant later he heard the key turn.

'Orl right!' muttered Ben, while he listened for her retreating footsteps and heard none; the soft carpet gave away no secrets. 'If it ain't going to be no comedy fer me, it ain't goin' to be one fer you, neither!'

He rebelled against her abrupt departure. She had not even stopped to switch on the light. He stretched out his hand for the switch, touched something cold, and jumped away. He jumped into something soft, and jumped back. The cold thing was merely the doorknob, and the soft thing was only the side of a bed, but in the dark all things are horrible when you are not feeling at your best. It took him five seconds to recover.

He stretched out his hand again, more cautiously this time, for he was not certain of his exact position and he did not want to establish abrupt contact with any other objects. His position being quite exact, he touched the doorknob a second time, proved its identity, and worked his fingers north-westwards. It was good navigation. The fingers came to port at another cold thing. The electric light switch.

'Got yer!' murmured Ben.

He worked the switch. His only reward was the sound of the click. No light came on.

'Narsty,' he decided.

Leaving the door, he carefully retraced his way to the bed he had leapt against. He wanted to sit down. His knees weren't feeling very good. But just as he was about to sit down—he was actually in process of descending—it occurred to him that somebody might be in the bed. This caused a rapid change of direction, and he sat down on the floor.

Well, for the moment, he would stay on the floor. When you're on the floor you have had your bump, and you can't bump any lower. Besides, by remaining where he was he would avoid the necessity of feeling the bed and perhaps finding something. Thus he took his rest on the carpet, and from this humble level set himself to think. His thinking shaped itself into a series of unanswerable questions.

'*Fust. 'Oo's this 'ere woman?*'

He stared into the darkness ahead of him, and the darkness remained uninformative.

'*Second. 'Oo am I?*'

He could make more progress here, though not sufficient. He was the dead bloke he had spoken to on the bridge. And the woman had engaged him for some job. But if she had never seen him before, and had to identify him by a skull-pin, where had she engaged him from? A Murderers' Registry Office?

'*Nex'. Wot is the job?*'

Murdering certainly seemed to be connected with it. Had she not told him so, in effect, on the doorstep? Of course, that might have been just a bit of back-chat. She was a puzzle, she was—no knowing how to take her. And then do you engage people to kill each other at so much an hour, like sweeping a room? Go on!

Just the same, she had implied that this was not going to be a comedy, and with that Ben very earnestly agreed. Whatever her job was, he had a job of his own, and he was going to hang on to it till kingdom come. And it probably would come. But he could not complete his job till he knew hers. So what was it?

The darkness refused to tell.

'*Nex'. Wot abart this journey?*'

Blank.

'*When's it goin' to start?*'

Blank.

'*Where's it goin' to be to?*'

Blank.

''*Ow am I goin' to git out o' this 'ouse, s'posin' I want to?*'

Blank.

'*Yus, and wot's goin' on in this 'ouse? That's the fust thing, ain't it? Wot's goin' on?*'

This time he received an answer startlingly, but though it was illuminating it merely threw light upon himself. A thin beam shot across the room, played on him for an instant, and vanished.

He leapt to his feet, to be out of its path if it reappeared.

He stood stock-still in the new spot to which he had leapt. For five seconds nothing happened. Then the beam shot across the room again, picked him out as before, and vanished as before. It was following him.

'Lumme, it's one o' them death rays!' he thought, palpitating. A second thought was more comforting. 'Then why ain't I dead? So I ain't!'

A sound outside the door switched his mind to a fresh unpleasantness.

'She's still outside!' he reflected. 'She's bin there orl the time, listenin'. Crikey, 'ave I bin torkin' in me think?'

The key turned. The door slowly opened. Once more the thin streak of light revealed Ben's features. Its source was an electric torch, held in the hand of a tall, thin, shadowy figure.

4

The Man in the Next Room

'Good-evening, Mr Lynch,' said a soft, effeminate voice. 'That is, I take it you are Mr Lynch?'

Ben also took it that he was, and struggling to conceal his fright, he replied, with hoarse gruffness:

'That's me!'

'It is a sweet name,' went on the soft voice. It reminded one vaguely of dressmaking. 'Almost too sweet to believe. So perhaps, after all, we need not believe it?'

'Eh?'

'I expect you have chosen it to indicate your habits?'

A thin, ghostly hand moved up to the speaker's collarless neck, engaging it in a pale and flabby clasp.

'The last one called himself Churchyard, but I always thought that was a grave mistake. It proved prophetic. Yes.'

'I s'pose you know wot yer torkin' abart?' inquired Ben.

The visitor's attitude was not balm to the spine, but at least he did not appear immediately menacing, and this circumstance assisted the process of recovery.

'You,' he answered. 'Mr Harry Lynch. You will look

charming one day in wax. Meanwhile, I am very pleased
to meet you in the flesh and to welcome you to our little
home. Do you like it?'

'Well, I ain't seen much of it,' remarked Ben.

'You will see more of it.' He had been standing in the
doorway, but now he suddenly entered, closing the door
quietly behind him. 'Perhaps more than you want, but that
is only a guess. I spend a lot of my time guessing. Life is
terribly boring, apart from its occasional highlights—yes,
there are occasional highlights—and you must fill in the
time with some occupation. Even staying in bed tires you,
after a certain number of hours. Once I played golf. Yes,
really. I got so I could hit the ball. But you can't play golf
here. So I guess. I guessed right about Mr Churchyard. Do
you mind if I examine you a little more closely? You seem
an unusually interesting specimen.'

Once more the electric torch—the only source of illumination—nearly blinded Ben.

''Ere, I've 'ad enough o' that!' exclaimed Ben.

'Yes, I hope you will forgive me for having used my
private peepholes. They are in the wall. My room is next
to yours. Isn't that nice? But it will be better—do you
mind?—if you speak a little more quietly.'

'Why?'

'Well, it's rather late, isn't it? Now, then, your face. Yes,
I do like it. Not classic, of course. Not aesthetic. But—as I
have already implied—manna for wax. And you can see
it on the front page of a newspaper, with interesting titbits
under it. I do a lot of reading.'

'Yus, well, that's enough abart my fice,' growled Ben. He
disliked the analysis, and he was sure Mr Harry Lynch
would have objected also. 'Wot abart *your* fice?'

'Oh, certainly.' The torch swung round, and the visitor's chin became grotesquely illuminated. Above the chin were a weak mouth, very pale cheeks, and light blue eyes. The crowning hair was yellow-gold; perfectly waved. 'Not your fancy, eh?'

'I saw worse once,' replied Ben.

'How you must have suffered,' sighed the visitor. 'Personally, I like my face. I spend a lot of time looking at it. My theory is that you either attend to your appearance, or you do not. No half-measures. I attend to it. My life is different from yours, but, having accepted it—and again there are no half-measures—I am quite as happy as you, or a politician, or a member of the Stock Exchange, before we all go to hell. Now tell me something else. This is important. What do you think of your hostess?'

'Ah, well, there you are,' answered Ben noncommittally, while trying to work out what Harry Lynch's opinion should be.

'Am I?' murmured the visitor. 'I wonder! I see you believe in caution. You may be right—especially to one who has not been introduced and who has peepholes in walls. Do you always sit on the floor, by the way? I may be a policeman. Only I am not a policeman. If I were, I should be very careful not to put the idea into your head. My name is Sutcliffe. No relation to the Yorkshire Sutcliffe. Cricket tires me. Stanley Sutcliffe. Sometimes our hostess calls me Mr Sutcliffe. Then I call her Miss Warren. Sometimes she calls me Stanley. Then I call her Helen. sometimes—in strict private—she calls me Stan. What I call her then is not for your ears. Are we better acquainted? I hope so. I am feeling rather tired, and want to get back to bed. I hope you like my dressing-gown. But what I am asking you is whether you like your hostess?'

'She's a good looker,' replied Ben.

'She is certainly a good looker. She has one look that is so good it melts me. Be careful.'

'It 'asn't melted me.'

'I don't expect you have seen it yet.'

'It won't melt me when I does!'

'I wish I could still paint. I used to, you know. Futuristic. But I gave it up. I found the brushes so heavy. I've given up a lot of things.' His pale blue eyes grew sad. 'I would like to paint you. I am sure we could startle Art between us. Your face *must* be preserved somehow!'

'Yus, well, we're torkin' of Miss Warren's fice,' Ben reminded him, secretly grateful for the valuable information of her name.

'Ah—Miss Warren's face,' murmured Stanley Sutcliffe. 'Yes. Miss Warren's face.' He closed his eyes. 'Dangerous, Mr Lynch. Dangerous. Why, even—' He paused, and opened his eyes. 'But it will not melt *you*, eh?'

'Nothink melts me,' asserted Ben. 'Not even when me victims 'oller!'

'Mr Churchyard made the same boast,' smiled Mr Sutcliffe sympathetically. 'Standing in the very spot you are standing in. "She can't make me do what I don't agree to do," he said. And he would agree to most. Then she came in—' He paused again, and turning to the door, directed his torch towards it. 'Well, well, we shall see. Of course, Mr Churchyard was not the first. In my own case, I made no boast. I just gave way at once. Much the simplest. I believe in ease. One day—if we're allowed the time—we must discuss philosophy.'

31

'P'r'aps yer could do with a bit,' suggested Ben.

'Perhaps I could, and perhaps I could not,' replied Mr Sutcliffe thoughtfully. 'And perhaps, after all, it would be a mistake to discuss it. Discussion is rather fatiguing, though, of course, one can always train. Well, now I have seen you and know what is on the other side of the wall, I shall return to my room. Good-night.'

''Ere, 'arf a mo'!' exclaimed Ben, quickly. 'If *you've* done, I've got a few things I'd like to ask!'

'Be sure they are few,' said Mr Sutcliffe, 'and don't count on getting answers.'

'Well—corse, I knows a lot,' began Ben, cautiously feeling his way. 'I knows I've bin engaged fer a job—'

'But you don't know what the job is,' interposed Mr Sutcliffe, helpfully. 'No. And you won't, till she chooses to tell you.'

'Meanin' *you* won't!'

'I certainly won't.'

'P'r'aps yer can't?'

'Perhaps I can't. Perhaps is such a useful word. It means nothing.'

'Oh, well—I can wait!'

'Since you will have to, that is fortunate. I have no doubt, Mr Lynch, that in your own slum, or castle, or service flat, or Soho restaurant, you are the monarch of all you survey—but there is only one monarch *here*!'

'Meanin' Miss Warren?'

'Meaning Miss Warren.'

'Well, I'm 'ere to do 'er instrucshuns,' said Ben, 'but she can't twist 'Arry Lynch rahnd 'er little finger!'

'She can twist Stanley Sutcliffe round her little toe,' confessed that individual.

'Then why ain't you doin' 'er job?'

Mr Sutcliffe seemed intrigued by the question. He considered it as though this were the first occasion it had occurred to him.

'I expect I am too gentle,' he replied, at last. 'I only know two or three ways of killing people, and of those only one is a certainty.'

'Oh! Well, what's wrong with the certainty?'

'No one knows anything about that but myself.' He suddenly frowned. 'And we don't talk about it . . . But the *real* reason,' he went on, changing the trend of the conversation, 'is that Miss Warren has other uses for me and likes me to remain at the flat. Do you know, Mr Lynch, I haven't been out for five months.'

'Go on!'

'It's the truth. And it's a pity. Or isn't it? Ease. Comfort. The pleasant passing hours. Omar Khayyám.' He held up a soft hand and moved the fingers contemplatively. 'I wonder whether I could still hit the ball?'

5

What the Morning Brought

Ben spent one of the most unpleasant nights of his experience, and the extent of the unpleasantness may be gauged from the circumstance that his nocturnal experience was vast, including coal-bunkers, luggage-vans, dustbins, water-tanks, and once a coffin.

When Mr Stanley Sutcliffe left the room, his strangely flabby atmosphere remained, hanging on the darkness like a nauseous scent. The possibility that his pale blue eye might at any moment be plastered against some invisible peephole assisted the illusion of his continued presence. Helen Warren, at least, was physically beautiful. She could give satisfaction to the senses if not to the soul. Mr Stanley Sutcliffe could not give satisfaction, in Ben's view, to anything. Not even to a golf ball.

'Wonner why she 'as 'im arahnd?' he reflected. 'Is 'e one o' them conternental giggerliots?'

Ben had been to Paris, and at a dance-hall had watched anæmic young men perform amorous revolutions with jewelled ladies, the latter usually stout and elderly; and when he had asked what these curious male creatures were, he had been informed. He liked a bit of French, so he had memorised the word.

'That's wot 'e is, a giggerliot,' he decided, 'and she keeps 'im shut 'ere case 'e runs away. Five months—lumme, no wunner 'e looks like Monday's cod!' A nasty thought followed. ''Ope she ain't goin' ter keep *me* 'ere five months!'

The probability was happily reduced by the reflection that he would make a very bad giggerliot.

After creeping to the door and discovering that Mr Sutcliffe had relocked it, Ben turned to the bed. The time had come to test it, because he did not want to spend the whole night—or what was left of the night—on the floor. If the spy-holes were used, the procedure would not reflect much credit on Harry Lynch, while even if the spy-holes were not used, the morning light, revealing a comfortable empty bed, would produce humiliation. So he felt his way carefully towards the spot where he believed the bed was, screwed up his courage, raised his fist, and brought it down hard. If anything *was* on the bed, he was going to get in the first whack.

He whacked air. A second effort, however, was more successful. He whacked a pillow. It yielded with pleasant obedience to his attack, as did the rest of the bedding when the attack was continued rapidly down its complete length . . . Good! Just a bed. Nothing nasty in it. That was all right, then!

He took off his boots. Or, rather, somebody else's. They had had quite half-a-dozen previous owners, and the last had discarded them into a ditch beside a dead cat. Ben had left the cat but had taken the boots. Morally one has a right to the surplus contents of a ditch, though technically they may be crown property.

He did not take off his collar because he hadn't one. It saved time. He did not take off his coat because it was next to nature, and it was risky to sun-bathe when anybody might pop in on you. The same applied to his trousers. Going to bed, with Ben, was taking off your boots; getting up, putting them on again.

He stretched himself out on the bed. Not in it. You can't spring so far when you take the clothes with you.

Nothing happened saving the constant expectation that something would. He listened for footsteps. He watched for the thin ray of light. The minutes slipped by in nerve-racking uneventfulness and silent blackness. Even the silence and the blackness contributed some special quality to the occasion. He had never known them so utter.

A thought began to worry him before he knew what it was. It materialised into: 'Blimy, I never looked *unner* the bed!'

After a period which he estimated at, roughly, ninety-five hours, he drifted into the companion torture of dreams. The last, characteristic of the rest, from which he awoke with a start may be recorded. He was dancing with a skeleton. The skeleton was wearing jewels, and he was the skeleton's giggerliot. Its bony arms pressed him so hard against its open ribs that they pressed him right inside, and he was struggling to get out when he opened his eyes and found Mr Stanley Sutcliffe smiling at him.

Mr Sutcliffe was still in his dressing-gown and, with the room, was fully revealed for the first time by the light of a bedside lamp.

'Oi!' gasped Ben.

'So you observed before,' answered Mr Sutcliffe. 'You say it beautifully.'

Ben screwed up his eyes and then opened them properly while Mr Sutcliffe continued:

'One day I must write some poems about you. Those I think I *could* do. Poetry is a sort of last resort when you've nowhere else to go. I wish I weren't so witty. Did you sleep well?'

'Wot 'ave *you* come back for?' demanded Ben.

'It's time to get up,' replied Mr Sutcliffe. 'I mean, for you to get up.'

'Go on!'

'Eight o'clock, Mr Lynch.'

Ben stared. If it was eight o'clock, which seemed impossible anyhow, why wasn't there some daylight in the room? And where had the lamp come from?

'You don't know what you're doing for me,' said Mr Sutcliffe. There was no enthusiasm in his tired voice, yet the words had a curious genuineness. 'You fit right into my hobby. Guessing, you know. I shall guess lots of things about you—till you drift away, like all the others, and become the big, final guess. Yes. But what I'm guessing now is small fry. I just look at your interesting face, and see if I can read behind. You won't mind if I study you a lot, will you? I'm reading *Alice in Wonderland* at present, but I find it rather stiff, and I shall put it aside for you. You're much nicer. And easier. You are wondering now about the light.'

'Gawd, talk abart talkin'!' muttered Ben.

'But am I right?' insisted Mr Sutcliffe.

'This time,' admitted Ben, 'but p'r'aps yer won't be *nex'*!'

'Well, we'll wait till the nex' comes, and meanwhile I will

satisfy your curiosity this time. A lamp is useless without those glass globe things. Last night your lamp didn't have one. This morning I have brought one, so it has.'

'Oh! Well, wot's wrong with drawin' the curtains?'

'Draw them and see.'

'Would you like to draw 'em for me?'

'I should dislike it intensely. I have already been on my feet for a long time for this early hour. I never walk or work unless I have to, and—you may as well know it at once—there is only one person in the world I take orders from, and even she occasionally makes me do more than I think is strictly good for me.' He stared at the carpet contemplatively. 'It was she who asked me to come in and wake you.'

'Yer mean, Miss Warren?'

'There is only one "she" here.'

'Well, wot 'ave I bin woke for? Breakfust?'

'But not, for you, in bed.'

'Oh!' It occurred to Ben that Harry Lynch was not asserting himself sufficiently, and he frowned. 'Well, I git up when I want to, see?'

'Really?' murmured Mr Sutcliffe, raising his faint eyebrows. 'Really? But that is most interesting. Only I am going to guess that you will be very, very wise, Mr Lynch, and will want to get up *now*.'

'Why?'

'Because what Miss Warren wants comes before what you or I want, and what she will want this morning at a quarter-past eight precisely is your presence. I assure you, *our* wishes, where separate from hers, are Also Rans.' He sighed. 'Also Rans. Dear old phrase. I still bet sometimes on paper. Last week I made £170. I think I must bet again today and lose it. Having so much money is rather taxing. Well, Mr Lynch, in a quarter of an hour. The second door on your left. The first is the bathroom.'

He turned to go, but paused at the door.

'And, by the way, Mr Lynch,' he added, 'if that is not your natural colour, I think I should wash.'

This time he did not lock the door after leaving the room. He left the way clear to the bathroom.

But before going to the bathroom to lighten his hue, Ben went to the window and drew aside the heavy curtains. The longed-for daylight that would have mitigated the suffocating atmosphere was blocked out by ironic boards. Now Ben understood the utter darkness and silence of the place.

Were all the windows in the flat blocked up?

The bathroom window was. He scrubbed by artificial light, and the passage by which he walked from his bedroom to the bathroom was illuminated by a soft glow of electricity from the hall beyond. No wonder the atmosphere was atmospherically as well as spiritually heavy!

'If that bloke's 'ad five months o' this without no sun,' thought Ben, 'corse 'e's barmy!'

The unusual ablutions over, he returned to his bedroom and wondered how long he had been out of it. He possessed no watch and he had heard no striking clock, and he was not good at guessing time. It was not going to be easy to hit a quarter-past eight.

'Say I was in the bedroom at four past,' he tried to work it out. 'Orl right. That's four past. Then say it took me three minutes fer each 'and and a couple fer the 'ead, and then one more when I dropped the soap. Well, that'd mike it—well, whatever it'd be, wouldn't it, so wot is it?'

He gave it up.

But help was at hand. The door suddenly opened and Mr Sutcliffe's head came round the crack.

'Fourteen past,' announced the head. 'She likes punctuality.'

Then the head disappeared. Mr Sutcliffe was a tired young man, but he possessed a languid nippiness.

At exactly a quarter-past eight, Ben knocked at the second door on the left. Miss Warren's voice, richly sleepy, bade him come in.

She was in bed. She wore a deep blue dressing-jacket and a deep blue boudoir cap. The boudoir cap reclined luxuriously against a soft pillow with lace edges, and she radiated an atmosphere of heavy, confident attraction. If there was any confusion, it was not on her side.

'Don't be bashful, Mr Lynch,' she remarked with a faint smile, after a short silence.

'Eh? 'Oo's bashful?' retorted Ben.

'I'm sorry, I've evidently mistaken your expression,' she answered. 'Never mind, we'll soon know each other better. Of course, we'll have to do something about your clothes. How did you sleep?'

'Not so bad.'

'And you needn't be polite, either. I like to know all my guests are thinking, though I can generally guess without being told. What are your complaints?'

'Well,' said Ben, 'fer one thing, I ain't uster sleepin' with me door locked.'

'And for another thing?'

'Bein' spied on! I bar that!'

'Who has been spying on you, Mr Lynch?'

'I expeck you know as well as me. The bloke in the next

room. 'Ow'd *you* like it if some 'un sent searchlights through peepholes onter *you*?'

'He will do it!' smiled Miss Warren. 'I'll speak to him about it. But the locked door—well, we'll see. And is that everything?'

'No,' replied Ben, refusing to be rushed. He was quite sure Harry Lynch would not have permitted it. 'I like a bit of air.'

'I see. The windows are worrying you, too?'

'Tork abart suffercatin'!'

'And how about the arrangement of this room? Do you think the bed would be better against another wall? And is the colour-scheme satisfactory? And your shaving-water— what time would you like it brought?' She was still smiling, but a quality that made Ben wary had entered her voice. Ben's difficulty was in finding a common denominator between what he felt and what Harry Lynch would have felt. He was struggling with the difficulty now as Helen Warren continued, 'Now, listen to me, Mr Lynch. I am going to admit at once that I find you a most unusual person, and that, when I have found out a little more about you—and I take no chances, you know—I think you will prove the very man for the difficult job you've been engaged for. Because of that I am ready to put up with your—peculiarities, shall we call them?—and as I like novel sensations I am even ready to enjoy certain of them. But while you are in this flat you will not question the rules of this flat—when your own sense cannot supply any reason—and you will keep to the rules of this flat. Now, is that quite clear?'

Ben returned her steady gaze for a little while without replying. 'She's watchin' me,' he thought, 'to see 'ow I'm tikin' it. So 'ow 'ave I gotter tike it?'

Conscious that the moment was a crucial one, he wished some invisible person could have been standing by to advise him. That dead detective, for instance, whose job Ben was carrying on—*he* would have known how to deal with this dangerous, soul-searching woman! Yes, and she was searching her new recruit's soul now, all right . . . Then, all at once, the new recruit remembered something.

Once, on a cannibal island, he had been taken for a god by the natives. He had maintained the convenient but uncomfortable illusion, actually using it for the betterment of the island before effecting his escape, by periodically pretending to himself that he *was* a god. Only by yielding to the part was he able to understand and act the part. Now he would have to yield, when in doubt, to the part of Harry Lynch, to discover how he would behave.

The mental gymnastics of slipping into the skin of a crook and potential murderer were less attractive than those of entering the more ethereal surfaces of a deity. The latter gave you a sort of a glow, like. The former gave you a sort of a shudder, like. 'Yer can't git away from it,' reflected Ben. 'I fair 'ates blood!' But it was for the blood of a dead detective he would now be assuming that red was his favourite colour, and that thought would sustain him.

'Don't keep me waiting, Mr Lynch, will you?' said the woman who was watching him.

'I do when I wanter,' replied Mr Lynch.

'Really?' She raised her eyebrows. 'Perhaps I'd better remind you, then, that your predecessor wanted to.'

'Prederwotter?'

'I must remember your dictionary is limited. The man I engaged before you.'

'Oh! Wot 'appened to 'im?'

'Something I hope will not happen to you.'

'I'll see it don't. I mike things 'appen to other people, and I knows 'ow to tike care they don't 'appen to me. Yer don't think yer've engaged Little Lord Fowntleroy, do yer?'

'I confess I don't see the resemblance.'

'I've twisted more necks than I can cahnt.' He looked at her neck. 'There was one they couldn't untwist. Orl right. That's me!'

Helen Warren may have been impressed, but she was not alarmed. Slipping her hand under the lace-edged pillow, she brought out a little revolver and laid it on the silk counterpane.

'And that's me. So now you know, Mr Lynch, what *will* happen to you if you don't keep to the rules of this flat. By the way, do you intend to?'

For an instant, while her firm slender fingers tapped the revolver—the murderous weapon made an incongruous gleam on the attractive counterpane—he almost forgot he was Harry Lynch, twister of necks, for he knew that Helen Warren was ruthless and would suffer no heart-pangs if she popped him off. But the instant passed, and a wave of personal indignation helped him to maintain the role he was playing.

'If you think I git palpertashuns when I sees a popgun,' he answered, 'yer wrong!'

'Which is not a reply to my question,' she observed. 'I asked whether you were going to obey the rules?'

'Yus, I know you did.'

'Well?'

'P'r'aps it derpends.'

'On what?'

'On if there's any more. 'Ave I 'eard them orl?'

'No, you have not heard them all,' she said. 'There are a few more.'

'Ah!' muttered Ben. 'Let's 'ave 'em!'

'You are not really a lady's man, Mr Lynch, are you?'

'I treat 'em right when they treat me right.'

'How fair! I am that way with people myself. Well, one of the rules you've not heard yet is that nobody leaves this flat without permission.

'Another is that, although I may permit others to be humorous, when it amuses me, the others must understand that I myself am quite serious.'

'Oh!'

'Another is that, if the lift-bell rings, I answer it.'

'That's O.K. I ain't bin engaged fer a butler.'

'You have been engaged, Mr Lynch, to do whatever you are told to do—which brings me to the last rule, and the reason why I have sent for you. You are receiving a pound a day retaining fee, free board and lodging till the time comes for your job, expenses during the job, and fifty pounds when you have completed the job. I don't think you will have to wait long. In fact, you may be sent on the job at any moment. But meanwhile I have a rule against idleness, and though you will not be my butler, you will be my cook and my waiter, and you will begin your duties at once by preparing breakfast for myself and Mr Sutcliffe. We take breakfast in our rooms. The kitchen is the first door on the right beyond the lift. You can't make a mistake, because all the other doors are locked. Can you make tea and cook eggs?' She laughed suddenly at his expression, and slipped the revolver back under the pillow. 'We're not going to quarrel, Mr Lynch. You'll find a pound note on the kitchen table, and a slightly more presentable suit than the one you are wearing over a chair. Profit by both, and bring in my breakfast in half an hour. Thank you.'

'Well, I'm blowed!' blinked Ben.

'If that's all you are, we needn't worry,' she replied sweetly. 'You can boil the eggs. Four minutes.'

Her tone bore a note of definite dismissal. He turned to go. But at the door he paused. What would Harry Lynch's attitude have been towards boiling eggs?

'Orl right, we'll carry on,' he said, 'so long as there ain't no 'ankey-pankey, and so long as I ain't done out of my proper job. But if you don't like my cookin', that's *your* funeral, see?'

'Close the door after you,' she answered.

Outside he nearly bumped into the pale Mr Sutcliffe. Mr Sutcliffe smiled, and put his finger to his lips.

'Yes, I was listening,' he whispered, without shame. 'I always do.'

'Corse, you don't know wot walls are for, do yer?' frowned Ben.

'I've heard,' smiled Mr Sutcliffe. 'They are to conceal us. To imprison us. To protect our little secrets. Terribly in the way. You did quite well, Mr Lynch. I wish you were staying longer. You can do my egg four-and-a-half minutes. Safer. And please, *please* cut the crusts off the toast.'

He slipped back along the corridor to his bedroom.

Trying to dispel an unpleasant idea that he had strayed into a lunatic asylum and that his job might be to polish off the worst cases when they arrived, Ben made his way across the hall to the first door on the right beyond the lift. The door led to the kitchen, the suit, and the pound note, as predicted.

Thoughtfully, he changed. In spite of the fact that the suit he changed to had holeless pockets and almost made him look respectable, he parted with his old clothes with regret. It seemed as though he were shedding the final remnants of his familiar personality.

The pound note in one of the holeless pockets soothed him a little. He felt he had earned it already, and if things got too hot and he had to escape, it would keep him for a month. Ben could live royally on eightpence a day. But he had no present intention of escaping. Imprisoning him more securely than locks and keys was the ghost of the dead detective, to which he was attached by an invisible chain.

He found the eggs in a small larder. Also tea, bread, butter, condensed milk, and other breakfast accompaniments. In a few minutes, the gas cooker was busy.

''Allo—wozzat?' he muttered suddenly.

A faint, buzzing sound had come from the hall. The lift? 'Well, it ain't my bizziness,' he reflected. 'I ain't on the door!'

He stared at the eggs reclining placidly in their hot bath, envying their placidity. He tried to think only of the eggs, but found he was thinking more of the lift. The buzzing sound came again.

'Ain't nobody goin'?' he wondered, nervily.

The eggs recaptured his attention for a few moments. How long had they been in? One minute or two? The lift had confused the count. Actually it was three.

Then he forgot the eggs again. Someone was in the hall; he heard a faint, filmy rustle. He also heard the dim whirr of the lift's ascent. Somebody was coming up? . . . well, why shouldn't somebody come up? . . . Only he hoped it wasn't another lunatic . . .

He crept to the door. The eggs continued boiling perilously. Curiosity beat him when he heard the lift stop and the gate slide aside. He opened the door a crack, turning the handle very softly, and peeped through.

At first he could see nothing but the back of a blue dressing-gown. Miss Warren was standing between Ben's nose and the lift, obscuring his view of the person who was just stepping out of it. But after a second the blue back made a little movement that was suspiciously like a start, and the movement altered its position. Now it was no longer between him and the lift, and he could see the person who had just stepped out.

Ben closed the door swiftly, his heart thumping. The visitor was a policeman.

6

Acid Test

The arrival of the policeman spelt the ruin of the eggs. They were now entirely forgotten in the graver problem that had suddenly presented itself.

'Wot's 'e come for?' speculated Ben anxiously. 'Yus, and 'oo 'ave I gotter be now? Lynch or meself?'

If the policeman had merely called to make inquiries he had called too soon. Apart from identifying the gang responsible for the detective's murder (with the actual murderer himself still absent), Ben could not assist, for he had not yet discovered the secret behind the crime. If, on the other hand, the policeman had called to make an arrest, would Ben's attempt to dissociate himself from the crime be successful? Was it not far more likely that he would be regarded as one of the gang, assuming the role of innocence to save his own skin?

'This is goin' ter be narsty,' decided Ben.

It was easy to guess how the police had got on the track. The chauffeur Fred had been caught, and had given away the address.

''Ere, git busy!' he instructed his numb mind as he stared at the door waiting for it to open. 'Wot am I goin' ted say when 'e arsks, "'Oo are you?"'

He imagined the policeman putting the question. Then he imagined himself replying, 'Bloke called Ben, see?' As that information did not appear enough, he had to carry the conversation a little farther.

'Oh, and who's Ben?' inquired the imaginary policeman.

'Chap wot's tikin' on a detective's job,' answered the imaginary Ben.

'Who's the detective?' asked the imaginary policeman.

'Well, I don't know 'is nime,' said the imaginary Ben.

'What's the job?'

'I can't say ezackly. See, I'm findin' aht.'

'When did the detective give you the job?'

'Lars' night.'

'Where?'

'On a bridge.'

'The detective wasn't *murdered*, was he?'

'As a matter o' fack, 'e was. We was jest fixin' things up when 'e was shot, so when the people wot shot 'im come along I pertends ter be one of 'em, like wot I was goin' to any'ow, so's I could git to know wot they shot 'im for. I'm pertendin' now, lumme, yer can twig that, carn't yer?'

Ben tried hard to make his imaginary policeman twig, but he failed miserably. Instead of twigging, the policeman responded:

'You're pretending all right, but it won't wash, Harry Lynch. You've got to come along to the station with the others.'

''Ere, don't be silly!' retorted the imaginary Ben. ''Ow can I be 'Arry Lynch? 'Arry Lynch was killed on the bridge afore the detective was!'

'Oh, no, he wasn't,' answered the imaginary policeman. 'The fellow called Ben was killed on the bridge before the detective was, and *you* killed him!'

Ben's brain reeled. He had imagined the conversation to the dizziest limit! Suppose the dead crook was really taken for himself—suppose he had got into the skin of Harry Lynch so tightly that there was no getting out of it? Well, in that case he would have to keep in it, until he had completed the job that would make the Big Five touch their hats to him, and could reclaim his own carcass!

'Yus, that's wot I gotter do,' he decided. 'I gotter go on bein' Lynch, and Gawd 'elp me!'

He donned a Lynch-like expression as the door suddenly opened and the policeman walked in.

The policeman was disappointingly large in the close-up, and his own expression, aided by a bristling moustache, was quite as forbidding as Harry Lynch's. Behind him stood Helen Warren and Stanley Sutcliffe, exchanging anxious glances.

'Now, then, let's hear *your* story!' began the policeman, without ceremony.

'Wot, 'ave I done somethink?' inquired Ben, affecting innocent surprise.

'What's your name?'

Just in the nick of time Ben saved himself from tripping over the first question. Harry Lynch would never give the police his name unless he had to. Gazing over the policeman's massive shoulder, he raised his eyebrows and asked:

'Wot's 'e wanter know for? Ain't yer told 'im?'

He watched Mr Sutcliffe pull a coloured handkerchief from his pocket as the policeman exclaimed truculently:

'You'll learn what I want to know for in two ticks, and never mind what they've told me. What's your name?'

'Brown,' said Ben, noting the hue of the handkerchief.

Mr Sutcliffe blew his nose appreciatively, but Ben's mind spun a little. He was Ben pretending to be Lynch pretending to be Brown. If Brown had to pretend to be anybody, he was lost!

'Brown,' repeated the policeman.

'That's it,' agreed Ben. 'Wot yer git at the seaside.'

'Are you trying to be funny?' demanded the policeman.

'Yus, I feel funny,' returned Ben, 'bein' hinterrupted in the middle o' me work!'

Was he showing the right shade of emotion, the correct degree of temper? It was a problem that would have puzzled the most acute psychologist and the cleverest actor, and Ben was neither. All he banked on was that Harry Lynch must have possessed a pretty sizable temper when it was aroused, but that Harry Lynch was smart enough to keep it under control when—like Ben—he was pretending to be somebody else. 'Yer know, wot I really want,' reflected Ben, 'is a nice long 'ollerday!' Which, unfortunately, was the very last thing he was destined to get.

'Oh, so you work, do you?' observed the policeman, glancing around.

'I 'aven't bin arst fer the weekend,' replied Ben.

'What sort of work?'

'Well, seein' we're in a kitching, I expeck it's shoein' 'orses.'

'How long have you been here?'

''Arf-a-nour.'

'Not in the kitchen, my man! Can't you answer a thing properly? In your job!'

'Well, 'ow am I ter know wotcher mean if yer don't speak pline?' grumbled Ben, again glancing over the policeman's shoulder for a hint of the answer that would not conflict with previous evidence.

He had a queer, uncanny sensation, as Miss Warren quickly raised two fingers, that he was being assisted by the spirit of Harry Lynch and that alone he would have shown less cleverness. It was a humiliating thought, although it was redeemed by the knowledge that he was using a dead man's brains to thwart his living associates.

'Take your time, won't you?' said the policeman.

'Well, I gotter think, ain't I?' retorted Ben. 'I've bin 'ere a cupple o' years.'

'Two years, eh?'

'Two was a cupple when I was a boy.'

'Since you know as much about two, let's get on to another sort. Ever heard of two o'clock?'

'Yus.'

'Can you tell me something about it?'

'Yus.'

'What?'

'Comes arter one o'clock.'

'Thank you. Did it come after one o'clock last night?'

Ben swallowed softly. Now they were getting to it!

'I suppose so! Wotcher mean? 'As some 'un put the clocks in reverse?'

'What I mean,' barked the policeman, 'is this. Where were *you* at *two* last night? And not so much looking over my shoulder this time, if you don't mind!'

''Oo's lookin' over wot?' grunted Ben, thinking hard. 'Ain't I ter move me neck?' The last word was not well chosen. The policeman appeared to be eyeing his neck speculatively. 'Two o'clock, eh? Well, corse, I was in bed.'

'Quite sure of that?'

'Yus. Tucked up warm.'

'Do you know where your mistress was?'

'Sime plice. Eh? Oh! I mean, a dif'rent one.'

'And—the gentleman now standing by her side?'

''E was in bed, too. Another dif'rent one. We got three.'

Miss Warren interposed. She appeared to judge it was time.

'Don't you think,' she said to the policeman, 'you ought to tell him why—'

'Kindly let me handle this in my own way,' interrupted the policeman. 'I know my job!' He spoke sharply, and turned back to Ben. 'Now, then, Mr—Brown! You say you were in bed last night at two o'clock.'

'Yus.'

'Tucked up nice and warm.'

'Yus.'

'Asleep.'

'Yus. No.'

'Which is it?'

'No! I wouldn't 'ave knowed it was two o'clock if I'd bin asleep, would I?'

'You'd have known you'd been asleep if you hadn't woken up.'

'Yus, p'r'aps, but I wouldn't 'ave knowed the others was asleep, so 'oo's the mug, you or me?'

'I see. Then you were awake?'

'That's wot yer are when yer ain't asleep.'

'What woke you?'

'Well, fust I thort it was a stummick-ache.'

'What did you think it was after?'

'It wasn't arter.'

'What do you mean?'

'Doncher unnerstand nothink I ses? I still 'ad the stummick-ache, and it was while I was still 'avin it that it thort it was somethink helse, that's pline enough, ain't it?'

In spite of the gravity of the situation, something very like a small titter emerged from the pale lips of Mr Sutcliffe.

'Make it a little plainer still, my lad,' answered the policeman frowning. 'What happened *exactly* at two o'clock, and don't waste any more time!'

'I won't if yer stop interruptin',' answered Ben. 'This is wot 'appens. A noise, see? I 'ears one. So I creeps aht inter the passidge. I goes ter the lidy's door. Orl quiet. But I couldn't 'elp worryin'—see, I'd 'ad a nightmare, it was that wot give me the stummick-ache, they git 'old of yer—so I jest opens the door a crack ter mike sure I can 'ear 'er breathin', and when I 'ears 'er breathin', which I does, I ses ter meself, "*She's* sife, wot abart the other one?" So then I goes ter '*is* door, and then I 'ears the noise wot woke me, 'e was snorin' with one o' them loud clicks.' The detective looked unconvinced, so Ben added, "E always does arter tinned salmon.'

Then a change came over the policeman. He stepped closer to Ben, and his voice tightened ominously.

'Now I'm going to tell *you* something, and see you don't interrupt,' he said. 'At 2 a.m. last night a detective was murdered on a bridge. He was shot, and a woman was seen picking someone up and driving away from the spot immediately afterward. She got clear, but we've been hunting all night, looking for clues, and this morning we've found her. Her name is Miss Warren. She is standing behind me at this moment with the man we believe she picked up. Identify him, and that will fix him as her accomplice in the crime. Naturally, smelling trouble, you did your best for your employers by inventing an alibi for them, but I don't expect you knew how serious the trouble was. We've got nothing on you, of course, and maybe we won't press you with any awkward questions if you just tell us the truth. You can't help them,' he concluded, 'because they are already under arrest, and the place is surrounded.'

Ben stared at the policeman. Then something happened inside him, and he punched the man on the jaw.

'You're a fine bobby, aincher?' he cried indignantly, as the policeman toppled back into Mr Sutcliffe's arms. 'Arrested, are they? And plice surrounded, is it? And corse, when the charge is murder, yer've never 'eard o' 'bricelets, 'ave yer? Not ter menshun yer mustache is comin' orf!'

Miss Warren smiled coolly as her chauffeur nursed his bruise.

'Your round, Mr Lynch,' she said, 'and when I tell you that you have passed your test—and that you'll do—perhaps you will forgive me for having made use of the disguise Fred has returned home in? I think you'd better cook some more eggs.'

7

The Signal Arrives

For three days, waiting for the signal that was to start him on his mysterious journey, Ben remained imprisoned in the silent, suffocating flat.

It was not completely silent. Their own footsteps along the soft-carpeted passages, their own voices modulated to the mood of an invisible conductor who favoured pianissimo, the occasional humming of Mr Sutcliffe ('I like music,' he once confided to Ben, 'but the full blast of my song went when I came here, so now I just hum'), and the opening and closing of doors, marked the minor events of an existence pregnant with expectant monotony; and the airless atmosphere was periodically alleviated by electric fans. ('The fans don't generate new air,' Mr Sutcliffe explained, 'they just push the old air about to prevent it from standing still and dying.') But there was a sense of stifling soundlessness. Nothing was contributed from outside. They lived in a tiny world of their own, a world of secrets, with the lid tightly screwed down lest the secrets should escape and burst.

The inmates themselves behaved with the organised calmness of those accustomed to sieges, although behind the calmness they reflected their separate moods and individualities.

Helen Warren's mood was that of a queen. Her word was law, and disobedience, if it came, surprised without disturbing her. She spent the mornings lazily and luxuriously in her bedroom, sending for her companions when she wanted them, and dismissing them peremptorily when she had had enough of them. She was notably less strict with Stanley Sutcliffe than with the other two, a fact which one of the other two resented. Ben soon discovered that Fred, the chauffeur, was jealous, and he had to admit himself that the fair-haired, smooth-cheeked 'giggerliot' received more than his share of privileges.

'Wot's the reason?' he asked Fred, braving the chauffeur's surliness. Fred never ceased to smart from the blow Ben had given him, and although he had not returned the blow he seemed to be waiting for the chance. 'I can't see anythink in 'im. 'E's more like a cod-fish than a man, if yer git me.'

'Why be so hard on cod-fish?' grunted Fred.

'Wot's 'e do 'ere?'

'Do we inquire what any of us do here?'

'So we don't,' nodded Ben. 'I see wot yer mean. But I wasn't speakin' crimernal. Is 'e one o' them, well, giggerliots?'

To this Fred made no response, either because he would not or could not.

In the afternoons there was an atmosphere of siesta, as though in reward for a morning of toil. As far as Ben could make out, the only one who toiled in the place was himself. Helen Warren reclined in the sitting-room and read French books. (French always seemed to Ben a suspicious language.)

Fred sat in an armchair, smoking and scowling. Mr Sutcliffe retired to his bedroom to study his face or manicure his nails. But tea brought him out again, in a brilliant red dressing-gown. He spent most of his life in dressing-gowns. After tea, cards were produced.

'Do you play cards, Mr Lynch?' Helen Warren asked him on the first occasion.

'On'y Jack o' Clubs,' he replied.

'I don't know that one.'

'It ain't differcult. The one 'oo draws the Jack o' Clubs goes aht and kills somebody.'

'How too, too sweet!' murmured Mr Sutcliffe, languidly taking a pack just as the chauffeur was reaching for it. 'Do you mind, Freddie? I lose so much when you shuffle.'

'If I had flabby fingers like your, I'd keep them hidden!' retorted the chauffeur, viciously.

As Ben noted the tiny tinge of colour that crept into Mr Sutcliffe's smooth cheeks he suddenly recalled, with a little shock, a remark which this strange young man had made to him: 'I only know two or three ways of killing people, and one of those only is a certainty . . . and we won't talk about *that*!' But the tinge of colour quickly faded, and the conversation ended as Miss Warren took the cards and cut for deal.

In the evening, after a dinner ordered by Miss Warren with an intelligent awareness of the cook's limitations, the cards were again brought out for a short game before an early retirement.

That, assumedly, ended the activities of the day. If things happened at night they were beyond Ben's personal knowledge, and merely lived in his imagination. They lived there a little too vividly.

It was during the fourth night beneath this sinister, heavily-pressing roof that the vividness of his imagination became almost unbearable. He had gone to bed wondering how much longer he could stand the nerve-racking atmosphere, and he had plunged almost immediately into a string of nightmares. His efforts to wake from them merely plunged him into worse ones. Skeletons in policemen's helmets, chauffeurs with scalping knives, a snake in a boudoir cap— all chased him in relentless succession, and when he tried to dive out of windows he found them boarded up.

But he was himself partially responsible for the most unpleasant nightmare of all. He heard a buzzing. The lift ascended. Out walked the Jack of Clubs. 'Hallo, Ben,' said the Jack of Clubs. 'You've drawn me.' Ben had fled to his bedroom. The Jack of Clubs had followed him, had dwindled to the size of a normal card, like the cards in *Alice in Wonderland*, and had plastered itself coldly on his forehead. It grew colder and colder, and pressed harder and harder, till suddenly Ben sat bolt upright in bed and found that the card was Mr Sutcliffe's hand.

'Gently, darling,' whispered Mr Sutcliffe. 'It's only Nurse come to wake you.'

Mr Sutcliffe looked like another nightmare. He was wearing a black dressing-gown.

'Wot's 'appenin'?' gulped Ben.

'Sh!' answered Mr Sutcliffe, softly. 'Someone has called.'

The lift had not been entirely a dream, then! But, of course, the caller could not really have been the Jack of Clubs.

'Oo?' asked Ben.

'I shall miss hearing you say "'Oo,"' sighed Mr Sutcliffe. 'You notice I am in mourning.'

''Oo's called?' repeated Ben.

'I think I must leave somebody else to tell you that. You see, my present visit is not official. I have wakened you as a friend.'

'Lumme, carn't yer answer a bloke?' muttered Ben. 'Is it the pleece? The real 'uns, this time?'

'It is not the police,' replied Mr Sutcliffe. 'Neither real or sham. The police never call here. Our hostess is much too clever. I would back her against anybody—even myself.'

Ben regarded the soft, slim figure in funereal silk.

'Beggin' yer pardon,' he said, 'I wouldn't back *you* agin' a flea with a toothache!'

'Not now, perhaps,' agreed Mr Sutcliffe sadly. 'Perhaps not now. But there was a time . . . Tell me,' he broke off suddenly, 'how are *you* with women?'

'Eh?'

'Do they worry you? Do they tear you? Can the sight of a knee—a particular knee, of course, not just any knee—can it sweep every other thought from your mind, and bring down your resolutions like a pack of cards?' He spoke with a queer intentness. He paused and considered. Thoughtfully, he continued, 'No. An amendment. Let us say—can it change your philosophy—your sense of values—your estimation of that abused term, Duty—your belief in Oliver Cromwell? I hope you are noting, Mr Lynch, that although I would put up a poor show against a flea with a toothache, I can still talk—still use good phrases—still show a brain. And that brain, reverting to a woman's knee that will one day crumble to dust, asks whether—meanwhile—it can open the gates that lead you into fields of lovely colours? Lovely scents? Lovely sensations? That make all else seem futile?' He paused again. 'Or are women just cattle?'

Ben broke a little silence to observe:

'Yer don't mean yer've stopped?'

'Yes,' nodded Mr Sutcliffe. 'It's your turn.'

'Well, I'm blowed if I know wotcher torkin' abart.'

'Then let us talk about something else. Your happy holiday here is over. You are going, as the fortune-tellers say, on a long journey. You had better get up.'

'But yer don't mean I'm goin' now? Ternight?'

'I think it highly probable. I did not let the visitor in, but I heard him arrive, and I caught a glimpse of him—very impressive—and I listened, as usual, at the door.' He held up a finger suddenly. 'Hark! Do you hear that soft metallic purr? My finger-nails are very bright tonight.'

'Eh?'

'Going—going—gone! Namely, the visitor. That was the lift descending. There is not a sound here I cannot interpret, not a silence I cannot read. If things were slightly different I would be a great man. Wait! Don't move! This is a tragic time. You are slipping away, Mr Lynch—slipping away. So solid now. And soon, just a memory! Did I talk to you? Did I touch you? Were you ever really here, with your "Eh?" and your "Oi"? I feel like Juliet.'

He vanished from the room. Ben got out of bed, feeling himself to make sure he hadn't melted yet. In less than a minute Mr Sutcliffe was back again.

'It is as I predicted,' he said. 'My visit now *is* official. You are to get up. You are to go to the second door on the left for the last time. Our Fred is also getting up. But he will return.'

'Don't *you* never git up?' grunted Ben, making for his trousers.

'I believe I did once last January,' replied Mr Sutcliffe,

'but I can't quite remember. Thinking backwards is so difficult.'

He departed once more. Ben dressed quickly. In the passage he saw a dim, stodgy figure gliding across the hall. It was Fred, going to the lift.

When Ben entered Miss Warren's room he found her sitting up in bed exactly as he had seen her on the first morning. Deep blue dressing-jacket. Deep blue boudoir cap. (He had seen that only a few moments ago in his dream.) Lace-edged pillow. Perfect picture of composure. Regarding her, Ben felt almost indignant at her attractive appearance at that time of night. 'Don't she never git messy?' he wondered.

'Well, Mr Lynch,' she began, in a businesslike manner, 'this time it's good-bye.'

'That suits me,' replied Ben, 'if the job's on.'

His heart was beating rather fast, for he was on the verge of learning the great secret at last, and once he knew that, he merely had to wriggle himself free and report to Scotland Yard. He managed to retain his outward composure, however, and to appear as composed as she.

'I thought it would suit you,' answered Miss Warren. 'This flat is hardly your natural environment. Your next lodging may be more appropriate.'

'Where's that?'

'Fred will take you there.'

'Yus, but where is it?'

'You will know when you arrive.'

''Ave it yer own way,' muttered Ben, concealing his disappointment. 'Wot's the job?'

'You'll know that later, too.'

The disappointment exploded.

'Ain't I ter know nothink?' he exclaimed. 'I s'pose I'll 'ear wot the job is arter I've done it!'

'You will hear before you do it,' Miss Warren promised calmly, 'and you will remember meanwhile that knowledge can be a dangerous thing.'

'Meanin' yer don't trust me! Yer puts me through wotcher calls a test with a bogus bobby ter see if I'll give yer away—I come through that O.K., didn't I—?'

'And you'll come through your job O.K., too,' she interrupted sharply, 'if you continue to obey orders in the future as you have obeyed them in the past. Not otherwise!' Her voice relaxed. 'Don't make trouble, Mr Lynch. Remember you were engaged on the definite understanding that you asked no questions, and only a few minutes ago in this very room I had to give my oath—to quite an important personage—that so far you had no inkling of your business.'

'Oh—did yer?'

'If I had not been able to give that oath, Mr Sutcliffe would not have wakened you up. The important personage, when he visited your bedside before Mr Sutcliffe did, would have made sure that you did not wake up at all.'

Ben swallowed quietly, and tried to get rid of another vision of the Jack of Clubs.

'So regard your ignorance as your protection, as well as ours,' she went on. 'When the time comes, your—particular genius will have full scope for its expression. Meanwhile, other minds will direct you—and watch you.'

'I see. The Jack—the himportant persernidge, eh?'

'I said *minds*.'

'Oh! Well, wot did the himportant persenidge come inter me room for?'

Miss Warren smiled.

'He couldn't quite believe my description of you. He wanted to be quite sure that you looked the right man for the job.'

'Yer carn't tell wot a man looks like with 'is eyes shut! Why didn't 'e wake me?'

'It suited him to see, but not to be seen. Well, I think that's all. Oh, no—something else. Money.'

'Yus, don't leave that out,' remarked Ben.

'You have already received three pounds. Mr Sutcliffe is waiting in the hall to give you five more, which will carry you on till the next instalment. I gather from something Mr Sutcliffe said that he wants to kiss you good-bye. Better not keep him waiting. You will forgive me if I myself am a little less effusive—though I admit,' she added, as she lay down, 'you have been refreshing. Good-night.'

She turned away, snuggling her head into her expensive pillow. But as Ben left the room he could not rid himself of the impression that she was still watching him.

Mr Sutcliffe stood waiting in the hall outside. He looked like a pale executioner in his dead black robe, and his doleful expression was equally indicative of the end of things.

'Here is largess for you,' he sighed, sadly presenting an envelope, 'and I am to tell you that your financial interests will be safeguarded all along the route—with, of course, the Big Plum at the end, provided you ever reach the end. Apart from that, my ignorance is as colossal as yours. Think of me sometimes. Oh, by the way, today I drove an apple into a saucepan with an inverted umbrella. Holed out in one. Record for the course. Still, it exhausted me. Now you have gone I shall have to fall back on horse-racing. Can you give me a tip for the Lynch Stakes? Perhaps one day, in return, I'll give you a tip for the Sutcliffe Stakes.' A queer look entered his eye for a moment, then vanished. 'Good-bye, Mr Lynch. Say something funny, please, to remember you by.'

'If yer think I'm feelin' funny,' answered Ben, 'it's one o' them roomers.'

'That'll do nicely,' replied Mr Sutcliffe, as he slid the lift gate open. 'Step inside, dear. Down for the basement bargains.'

A moment later Ben was alone, descending the narrow shaft to his next adventure.

8

Northward through the Night

Fred was waiting at the bottom. His attitude, as usual, was surly.

'Thought you were never coming!' he grunted, as Ben emerged from the lift. 'Think we've got all night?'

'Wot I like abart you,' answered Ben, 'is yer so cheerful.'

'Now, then, don't waste time!' snapped the chauffeur.

''Oo's wastin' time?' retorted Ben. 'You're standin' there grumblin', not me!'

'You've got some bloody cheek!'

'If I told yer wot *you'd* got, I'd still be torkin' next Christmas!'

A black coupé stood by the curb. Postponing further argument, they entered, and a few moments later were gliding swiftly through the dark streets.

For awhile they were as silent as the roads they travelled. The chauffeur was in no mood for conversation, while Ben was busy with his thoughts. But presently it occurred to Ben that perhaps he was missing an opportunity, and that it might be worth while trying to pierce the sultry atmosphere,

even at the expense of a little pride. Before long he would
be deposited in some new world, equipped only with ignorance. The ignorance may have saved his life in the flat, but
outside he preferred the protection of a little knowledge.

Whether Fred would supply the knowledge was another
matter. Certainly it would be impossible to pump the surly
chauffeur unless his unbending mood were altered.

'Got a new car, I see,' remarked Ben presently,
attempting to effect the transformation. 'Buy it out of
yer pocket-money?'

Fred made no reply.

'I never 'eard wot 'appened to the old 'un,' he tried
again. 'Did yer leave it in a ditch, like wot she told yer?'

Equally ineffective.

'Pity yer so chatty,' murmured Ben, giving up.

'I suppose *you* couldn't stop talking?' growled the
chauffeur.

'Easy,' answered Ben. 'But yer a mug. I was jest goin'
ter tell yer somethink Miss Warren said abart yer afore I
left 'er room.'

After a moment the chauffeur bit.

'What was it?' he asked curtly.

'"If yer wanter git on in the world," she ses, "watch wot
Fred does and do the hoppersit."'

That ended the conversation for a hundred miles.

During the hundred miles Ben concentrated on trying to
keep awake. There were several good reasons for the effort,
one being that he wanted to have some check on the time,
distance, and direction when he got to the other end—he
deduced they were travelling north—and another being
that he wanted to keep a check on his companion. He did
not imagine the chauffeur would do him any bodily harm,

for Ben was travelling under the protection of his mission—but you never knew, did you? In a sudden wave of emotion Fred might fling open a door and tip his passenger out!

But after awhile resolution began to weaken, and the strange lullaby of speed and night played on his frayed senses. Gradually the dark lanes dissolved into bottomless pools of blackness, the car lost its imprisoning solidarity, and Ben's soul escaped into the confusion of limitless space. This would have mattered a little less (though it would still have mattered; Ben loved an anchorage) had the Jack of Clubs not escaped with him. Together they floated about nocturnal cosmos in uneasy collaboration, till they descended into a vast, salty ocean.

Salt was everywhere. Salt and sea. Or was it salt and river? Or was it merely creek? Yes, probably it was creek, choked with weeds and grasses, for that would explain the decreasing speed . . . and the speed was undoubtedly growing less. . . .

He opened his eyes with a guilty jerk. The Jack of Clubs resolved into the form of Fred, the chauffeur.

It was still dark, but the inky outlines of small scattered buildings, and one tall spire pointing a ghostly finger heavenwards from a flat black earth, were faintly visible. Ben's nose, doing duty for his eyes, informed him that he was in a land of dikes and marshes.

A damp chill in the air added to the general sense of desolation.

'Don't worry, you're still alive,' came the sarcastic comment in his ear.

'If I wasn't, you wouldn't be fer long,' answered Ben, groping back towards consciousness.

'That's the only reason you are,' said the chauffeur.

They slid slowly through the outskirts of a little town. Presently, after two or three twists, the car stopped.

''Ome?' queried Ben.

'Near enough,' replied his companion, and handed him an envelope.

'Wot's this?' asked Ben, warily.

'Open it and see,' answered the chauffeur. 'It won't bite.'

'We do love each other, don't we?' said Ben, as he opened the envelope and extracted a sheet of paper.

The paper was headed, 'Further Instructions,' and Ben read them by the light above the control board:

'You are now in Boston, Lincolnshire.

'You are no longer Harry Lynch. You are Charles Wilkins, looking for work.

'You have not been in a car. You have walked from London, and you are dog-tired.

'You will knock at the door of a cottage pointed out to you by Fred. Fred will not accompany you to the cottage, and you will not knock till he has gone.

'There will be a light in a window of the cottage. That will explain why you have ventured to knock.'

At this point Ben raised his eyes instinctively from the sheet and glanced through the windscreen along the road. The car's lights were out, but a faint beam of yellow radiance streaked across the road from a dark smudge some fifty yards ahead on the right. He lowered his eyes to the paper again, and continued:

'A man with grey hair and a grey moustache will open the door to you. Tweed suit.

'You will explain your position to him. He will accept your story without question.

'He will make a suggestion. You will agree to the

69

suggestion. It will concern a place beginning with the letter M. You will then leave the rest to him.

'He will tell you in due course that his name is Smith, but do not address him as Smith until he has told you.'

('Some 'un thinks I'm a mug!' reflected Ben.)

'Speak to him always as Charles Wilkins, never as Harry Lynch. He has never heard of Harry Lynch, so will be unable to satisfy Harry Lynch's curiosity.

'Read these instructions through until you know them thoroughly, and them burn them in the presence of Fred.

'Remember that invisible eyes are watching you.'

With this veiled threat the instructions ended.

Ben read them through carefully three times, and then looked up to find the chauffeur holding a lighted match.

'Carry on,' said Ben.

The chauffeur applied the match to the paper. Ben held the paper till the little flame reached his corner, then dropped the corner and put his boot on it.

'O.K.' said Fred.

'Sime 'ere,' replied Ben. 'And now, I s'pose, orl we gotter do is ter kiss.'

'The cottage,' answered Fred stiffly, 'is the first one along the road on the right. You can see the light from here.'

'Thank yer fer nothink,' returned Ben. 'I've seed it already.'

The chauffeur stretched his arm across Ben and unfastened the door. Ben was assisted out by a sudden, vicious shove. As he picked himself up from the ground the car swung round. But Ben picked up a stone as well as himself, and smashed the windscreen with it while the car was gathering speed.

''Ave a nice warm journey 'ome, Sunshine!' he called.

And then turned towards the cottage.

9

Mr Smith, of Boston

With a sensation that he was getting farther and farther from his spiritual as well as his geographical base, Ben walked along the dark lane towards the ray of light that streaked across the road. He did not walk quickly because, although he had memorised his instructions, he still had a little thinking to do. In addition, a slow pace was consistent with the alleged fatigue of Charles Wilkins, unemployed.

'Let's git this straight,' he communed with himself. 'Now I'm Ben pertendin' ter be 'Arry Lynch pertendin' ter be Charles Wilkins, and the chap I'm doin' this larst pertend to ain't never 'eard o' the fust two. Orl right. 'Arry and Ben go back in the box. But is the chap I'm goin' ter pertend to goin' ter do any pertendin'? 'E expecks me, so 'e knows somethink's up. Is 'e really Smith, or is 'e Robinson pertendin' ter be Lloyd George pertendin' ter be Smith? Arsk me another!'

Havng reached this unsatisfactory point, he asked himself another.

'Wot sort of a bloke is this Charlie Wilkins to be? I gotter think 'im aht, ain't I? Nice or narsty? I 'ope there ain't a real Charlie Wilkins, else I'll be 'ad up fer libel! Corse, there was a real 'Arry Lynch, but 'e's dead so that don't count. Better mike 'im nice, ter be on the sife side— then if I'm 'ad up I can say I was doin' 'im a good turn. Right, 'e's nice. Quiet like. Should I mike 'im funny? No, don't think I'd be any good at that. 'E might like riddles.'

Then an idea struck him that, by its simple brilliance, made him stop dead.

'Lumme, I'm out o' work, ain't I?' he thought. 'Corse, not countin' me present job. And this Smith bloke's never 'eard o' Ben! Why not be me, and 'ave done with it?'

The immediate future brightened. The cloak of complexity fell from him. Charles Wilkins should be like Ben, and the actor would act himself!

He resumed his way in a happier frame of mind.

Reaching the ray of light, he paused in it, donned his most fatigued expression (it was not difficult), and turned towards the cottage, wondering whether Mr Smith was looking out. The fatigued expression was to cover that possibility, and so was the little scene that followed.

'Lumme, I'm fair done in!' he muttered loudly. 'Don't seem as if I can walk another step! 'Allo, wot's that? A light? Somebody's up!'

He stared at the cottage window. He decided to totter. He tottered. He did it so realistically that he fell over. 'I'm blowed!' he thought, as he picked himself up. 'I b'leeve I'm really done in!'

Aloud he said:

'P'r'aps they'd let me in if I knocked? When I tell 'em 'ow fur I've walked. Orl the way from Lunnon. That's right. 'Unded and somethink miles, and not a car to give yer a lift. I'll 'ave a shot any'ow.'

He staggered to the front door. Once you start acting ill, it grows on you. He knocked. The seconds immediately after he had knocked were not pleasant. Suppose, after all, this was not the right cottage? Or suppose it was, and the whole thing was a trap? They might have found out he was double-crossing them, and planned this visit to get rid of him. Mr Smith's suggestion might be to lie down and have a knife stuck through his middle. 'Body Found in Boston.' 'Body with a Hole through it.' 'Police looking for the Legs.' Lugubrious posters flitted through his mind while he waited.

Then the door opened, and an elderly man with grey hair and a grey moustache stood before him.

For a few moments they stared at each other with mutual suspicion. Then the man said, rather curtly:

'Well, what d'ye want at this time of night?'

'Saw yer light, guv'nor,' replied Ben. 'I'm fair done.'

'I'm sorry, but what can *I* do about it?'

'Thort p'r'aps yer might be a Christian and give me a crust or somethink.'

'What made you think that?'

'Took a charnce, guv'nor.'

'I see. And you're hungry?'

'That's a fack.'

The elderly man peered closer at his visitor. 'What's your name?'

'Wilkins, sir. Charles.'

'And your work?'

'Any I can git. One o' the unimployed, see? Walked from Lunnon.'

'That's a long way.'

'Yus, sir.'

'A very long way.'

'Yus, sir.'

'What made you come all that long way?'

'Lumme, ain't 'e corshus!' thought Ben as he answered, 'Well, see, I was told there was more work goin' in the north, but I ain't come across it. I don't s'pose you know of a job, sir? I can clean knives.'

'Knives,' repeated the elderly man. 'Knives.' The word seemed to have a vague fascination for him. 'Well, perhaps— come inside, anyway. Maybe I can find you something to eat. Though, mind ye, it's late, it's late.'

He stepped back into the passage, and Ben entered.

'Close the door, and come in here,' ordered the elderly man.

'I was lucky ter find yer up,' said Ben, as he obeyed.

'This way. In the parlour. Ay, you were. But I've a little business . . . often stay up after wise folk are abed. Now, then. Let's see.'

He spoke in a nervy, disjointed manner, though his eyes were placid. Going to a cupboard, he opened it, and gave a little exclamation.

'Ah! Just what we want!' he said. 'Just what we want. Bread—butter—cheese—you eat cheese?—and a knife.' He produced the items as he mentioned them. 'You can clean the knife when you have finished with it. Now, then, fall to. But not too fast, if you're famished, or you'll get pains.'

'Very kind of yer,' murmured Ben, securing the knife first. He preferred it in his own hand.

'Not at all—I'm always sorry for the unemployed,' answered his host. 'I have been unemployed myself— though now I have a little business. Oh, ay, I mentioned that. By the way, my name is Smith. Mr Smith, of Boston. Not that this is of any importance to you. To you I am merely a Good Samaritan who is providing you with a meal. There's water in that jug over there—I'm sorry it's all I can offer ye, but I'm teetotal. If you're not, I advise it. Now I'll leave ye for a bit, and come back when you have finished . . . Arrangements to make . . .'

He left the room. Ben made hay while the sun shone. Mr Smith returned in ten minutes, and raised his eyebrows.

'I see you do like cheese,' he observed. 'Well, it's made to be eaten. Now, then, about this job.'

'Yer don't mean yer've got one fer me?' asked Ben.

Mr Smith's eyes were on the window. The streak of light across the road was not quite so distinct. The first hint of dawn was beginning to banish the blackness of the night.

'No, I don't mean I've got a job,' replied Mr Smith. 'They don't grow on bushes like blackberries. But—I wonder—I think I know a good district.'

'Yer mean, not in Borston?'

'No. Not in Boston.'

'It ain't fur off, is it, sir?'

'Would that matter? Work is work, and you want it.'

'Well, I was jest thinkin', would I 'ave another walk?'

'Ah, I see. It so happens that—I wonder—now, I wonder—'

He paused. Ben thought, ''E ain't wonderin', 'e knows orl the time. Why don't 'e git on with it? Funny 'ow 'e gits on me nerves.'

'I'm afraid it's a long way off,' said Mr Smith. 'In fact, in Scotland. Muirgissie . . . You know it?'

'Never 'eard of it,' Ben assured him.

But he had heard of the initial M, and the name of Muirgissie completed the proof, if completion were necessary, that he was on the right track.

'Ay, the last time I was in Muirgissie, I was told there was work going,' Mr Smith resumed. 'I forget what. Farming, would it be? Or building? maybe building. Yes, I think it was building, but you must remember, Mr Wilkins, that I am not sure. Really, I know nothing about this work, nothing at all—no more, for that matter, than I know about you. It is for you to decide, not me, whether you would care to undertake the—er—risk of going to Muirgissie. You have called here in the night. I hear your story. And I make the suggestion. Well?'

'Yus, 'e's corshus orl right,' thought Ben. 'Won't tike no rersponserbility!' Aloud he said, 'I've on'y one thing agin' the suggestion, sir.'

'What is it?'

''Ow am I goin' ter git there.'

'Ah, now that is where I come in,' exclaimed Mr Smith. 'In a short while—in a few minutes, in fact—I am starting for Muirgissie. I have a little business in the neighbour-hood. Scottish connections and so on. Are you surprised that I should be going there? Come, come, why? It is because I go there—not often, I admit, but now and again, now and again—yes, that is how I hear of local conditions, and I mention them to you *because* I am just going there. Now would ye call that a coincidence, Mr Wilkins? And surprising that, as you have walked all the way from London, I should offer you a lift?'

'Everythink jest like yer say, sir,' answered Ben.

'Then provided you say the same, what more is there to wait for? The car is ready in the garage. If we start at once, we can have covered several miles by sunrise. Sunrise—the best time of the day—don't you think?'

He switched out the light as he spoke. In semi-darkness they made their way to the little garage beside the cottage. Two minutes later, Ben was travelling north again in a prehistoric Ford.

10

Exit Mr Smith, of Boston

The journey from Boston to Muirgissie was very different from the journey from London to Boston. It was twice the distance, and it was accomplished at half the pace. It was undertaken in daylight, from the first greyness of morning to the first greyness of night, and the country through which the ancient Ford passed lacked the convenient flatness of England's Eastern counties. When Lincoln lay behind, hills rose; before Scotland was reached, the hills became mountains, which seemed to Ben to grow higher and higher, and grimmer and grimmer, and lonelier and lonelier with each new range.

But in one particular the two journeys possessed a similarity. Conversation was at a discount, and the hours passed silently saving for the various voices of the gears. At his cottage Mr Smith had been spasmodically voluble, but the nervous energy that had propelled his words was now diverted to propelling the car, and it soon became evident to Ben that Mr Smith was propelling his car for all he and the car were worth, with possibly a little bit over.

'Whippin' the 'old 'orse, aintcher?' Ben ventured once, as they chugged fiercely up a hill.

'What?' answered Mr Smith.

The chug had drowned Ben's voice.

'I sed she'll blow up,' he roared.

'Ay, she'll go up,' replied Mr Smith.

You couldn't continue that sort of thing, so Ben relapsed into silence again.

They did not get out for meals. At midday they stopped in a lane to munch sandwiches and to wash the sandwiches down with tea out of a thermos. At four o'clock they repeated the process, in a valley. After tea Mr Smith began glancing about, and he redoubled his efforts.

'Anythink wrong, guv'nor?' inquired Ben.

'What should there be wrong?' retorted Mr Smith.

'No good arskin' me, but the noise she's makin' I thort she might 'ave sprung a sprocket or somethink.'

'Do you know what you're talking about?' demanded Mr Smith.

'No,' admitted Ben.

Later, however, he was convinced that something was wrong, though he was still uncertain whether the trouble were inside or outside his companion's brain. Mr Smith's nervousness increased painfully, and at last he stopped on a narrow moor road. There was not a habitation or, apart from themselves, a person in sight.

'Is this Muirgissie?' inquired Ben.

'Eh? No, of course not!' snapped Mr Smith. 'But it's not far now—I'm just thinking.'

'That's orl right,' answered Ben. 'I'll look at the scenery.'

The scenery was hardly more soothing than Mr Smith. They had halted on the verge of another deep dip, which somehow seemed to Ben particularly sinister. What lay in the dip? The cause of Mr Smith's anxiety? Beyond the unseen contents mountains rose again, their bases already smudgy with evening shadows, their heights glowing with unnatural colour. A gleam of water flashed somewhere. If there was a road through the mountains, Ben could not see it.

'Yes, yes, I think that's the idea,' muttered Mr Smith presently, to himself.

Ben waited for the unfolding of the idea. Mr Smith scratched his nose, then turned to him.

'I think, perhaps, it will be best for ye to get out now, Mr Wilkins,' he said.

'Wot—walk agine?' exclaimed Ben.

'Yes, and I will tell you why,' continued Mr Smith. Ben would have taken any odds that he was not going to hear the real reason. 'Why did I take pity on ye? Why have I gone to all this trouble for ye? Ay, tell me that? It was because you turned up tired. "Done in," you said. Walked from London. Now, if you had arrived at my cottage by car, would my sympathy have been aroused? Is that so likely?'

'P'r'aps not, sir,' admitted Ben.

'Very well, then!' There was a little note of relieved triumph in his voice. 'There we are! If you arrive in Muirgissie by car, you will deprive yourself of your best chance of help from—from the next person. You want work? You are not likely to get it if you drive up like a millionaire.'

If the ancient Ford possessed a soul, it must have smiled at the unexpected compliment.

'You agree?' asked Mr Smith.

'Wot you ses goes, sir,' replied Ben. 'O'ny I 'ope I ain't gotter walk far?'

'No, no. Perhaps a mile or two. Of course, if you are pressed—if someone has seen us together—you could say you had received a lift. A short lift. But, to volunteer it—why?'

Ben considered for a moment. On the whole, perhaps he was not sorry to shake off Mr Smith, but the absence of his present companion would throw him back on his own initiative again, and he could not steer the ship unless the departing pilot gave him some navigational instructions.

'Are you goin' on a'ead o' me?'

'Ay. To do that little business of my own I mentioned.'

'Oh, I see. Well, wot 'appens if I meet yer in Muirgissie?'

'Ah, I don't think that is very likely. My business is not in Muirgissie—I mean, not actually in the place itself—and it will only take a short time.'

'Yus, but where's this 'ere work? I've gotter arsk some 'un, ain't I?'

'Of course—I'm not forgetting that. There is an inn at Muirgissie. It's called the Black Swan. Black Swan. You can remember that?'

'If I try 'ard.'

'Go there and inquire. The innkeeper will know if there is any work going. Tell him your name, of course.'

'That'll 'elp?'

'Eh? Well, it won't do any harm. I think I'd mention it. Gives confidence, you know.'

'Oh! And that's the lot?'

'No, just one other thing,' answered Mr Smith. 'The post office. No one will know your address here. Well, how can they? And if you get work, you may be moving about. But one can always call for letters at the local post office.'

'Ah! Some 'un goin' ter write ter me?'

'How do I know? I know nothing about you or your affairs—nothing whatever. But if you think anybody may write to you, I am just telling you that you can call each day at the post office—and perhaps it would be as well ... What is that? You have dropped something!' He stooped suddenly, and rose with a small card in his hand. 'It must have slipped out of your pocket. You will want that, for identification, when you call at the post office.'

Ben took the card. On it was printed, 'Mr Charles Wilkins.'

'One o' them quincidences,' he commented dryly.

'Ay, very odd. Well, I think that's everything. Excepting, of course, that you will not mention anything about me, or this trip, unless you have to. You can't lose your way. There is only one road. You will be there in half an hour.'

Ben accepted the cue, and alighted. As Mr Smith prepared to depart, Ben suddenly grinned.

'I nearly forgot ter thank yer,' he said.

'Not at all, not at all,' replied Mr Smith. 'I—er—well, good luck.'

The car moved on. It descended into the dip and was swallowed up.

Lighting a cigarette—the best thing Mr Smith had done was to present him with a packet during the journey, and he had four left—he followed leisurely in Mr Smith's wake. He was in no hurry, and his anxiety to reach Muirgissie did not increase as he went down the narrow, winding hill and entered the region of shadows. If the half hour were spun out to an hour, he wouldn't cry about it. Until he reached the Black Swan, he was his own master again, and the sensation, while smoking a complete Gold Flake from end to end, was pleasant.

It was so pleasant, in fact, that Ben passed through the first period of wavering since he had entered a silent London flat with the intention of carrying on the work of a dead detective. He had eight pounds in his pocket. So far he had not had to spend a penny of his earnings, and those eight pounds would last a man who could sleep under the stars and eat with his fingers, eight months. What about losing himself for half a year? If it was cheating, his employers themselves were cheats!

It is to his credit that he decided to see the matter through before he remembered the sinister suggestion of his employers that he was being watched by invisible eyes. This suggestion had been made to him both verbally and in writing, and it occurred to him that to lose himself would probably be an impossibility, even in this lonely district. 'They'd 'ave me,' he reflected, gloomily, 'so I might as well go on. Besides, I sed I was goin' ter stick it, didn't I? Orl right!'

The road continued to descend and to wind. It was pouring itself off the moor into a black saucepan. Not a round saucepan, though. A long one, with a smudgy bottom. The smudges were shadows. In a valley night comes fast, slipping along like a dark tide.

But before the dark tide had completely enveloped the lane, Ben received a shock. Had the tide come a little faster, he would have been spared it. He had been walking, he reckoned, for about a mile and a half when he noticed another lane descending from another part of the moor, and forking into his. Reaching the point where the two lanes joined into one, he turned his head idly and glanced up the second lane. A dark object blocked his view.

Despite the fact that its outline was blurred by shadows

he recognised it immediately as a car, and a moment later he also recognised the car. It was the ancient Ford he had lately ridden in.

'That's rum!' he thought. ''As 'e bin ter Muirgissie already and come back? And wot's 'e stopped for?'

He was looking at the back of the car. It was heading uphill in the direction of the moor. Would Mr Smith welcome his intrusion if he approached? The Boston man had been anxious to separate himself from Ben and to end the association as completely as possible; still, nobody was about, and he might be in trouble.

'Better 'ave a squint,' he decided. 'Mindyer, I don't like the bloke, but if 'e wants a 'and, well, there yer are.'

He found Mr Smith sitting in the car, staring ahead of him. Ben stared, also, but couldn't see anything.

'Wot's up?' he asked.

Mr Smith paid no attention to him, but continued to stare.

'Oi! Wot's up?' repeated Ben. 'See a ghost?'

But it was Ben who was looking at a ghost. For the second time within a week, he found himself talking to a dead man.

For a few moments it just seemed impossible. While he knew it was true, his logic informed him that it could not be. Once, yes. On a bridge in London. But not twice—and the second time on the edge of a moor in Scotland. Over three hundred miles away. Oh, no! Why, even if such a thing could happen twice over, it wouldn't happen both times to the same man. Fate would choose another victim for the second dirty trick!

Then logic faded, and fact remained. However you argued, there was the fact—sitting back in the driver's seat and gazing ahead with unseeing eyes. And even logic returned presently, ruthlessly condemning its previous faults. These were not two isolated occasions in which Ben had been selected to participate. They were links in the same chain. The chain stretched from the bridge in London to this spot in Scotland—and beyond, to the Black Swan at Muirgissie!

Gradually, as Ben stood transfixed—last time he had leapt, but this time he felt glued—the gathering darkness completed its work and blotted the gruesome sight out. But he knew it was still there, just a few feet behind the intangible wall of blackness; that he could still touch it, if he stretched out his hand; and that the morning light would revive its vividness, developing it into stark solidarity once more . . .

"'Ere, this won't do!' he told himself. 'I gotter do somethink!'

The only question was—what?

Report the matter at Muirgissie? 'Fahnd 'im dead in the car, jest like that. No, I dunno 'oo 'e is—never seed 'im afore.' 'That's odd, for somebody saw you in the car with him.' 'Oh, yus, that's right, I fergot. 'E give me a short lift.' 'A short lift? Somebody saw you together near Boston.' 'Oh, yus, that's right, 'e drove me from Borston, so 'e did.' 'Where was he taking you to?' 'Muirgissie.' 'Why didn't he reach Muirgissie? Why did you get out before Muirgissie? Did you quarrel? What are those eight new one-pound notes doing in your pocket? And who are *you*, anyway?'

Such a cross-examination as this resolved behind a damp forehead, and it led to only one culmination—the arrest of Ben, alias Lynch, alias Wilkins, for the murder of Mr Smith, of Boston . . . if he reported the murder of Mr Smith, of Boston.

'Well—s'pose I don't?' he reflected.

In that case, he would leave Mr Smith where he was. He would proceed as though he had not turned his head at the forked road—'and arter orl,' he argued, 'I mightn't 'ave, mightn't I?'—and he would complete his interrupted journey to the Black Swan.

Perhaps the Black Swan would not prove quite as black as it sounded. Perhaps he would find it a temporary sanctuary in which he could at least bathe his head and see if that did any good.

'There's one thing, any'ow,' he thought. 'When things is so bad they can't git worse, well, they can't git worse . . . 'Allo! I'm movin'!'

Unconsciously he was putting the second alternative into operation, and was walking again towards Muirgissie. When his head failed, his legs often decided for him.

11

At the Black Swan

A girl stood under the faintly creaking sign of the Black Swan as Ben came round a corner and entered the single straggling street of Muirgissie. But for the light of a window behind her, she would have been invisible against the gloomy background of the inn. The light, a dim glow percolating through a thin red curtain, outlined her golden hair, and the curve of her neck, and the top half of her neat, attractive figure.

Just as, a few minutes earlier, Ben had not been able to believe in the dead Mr Smith, of Boston, so he was now unable to believe in this live girl of Muirgissie. She should not have been neat and attractive. She should have been untidy and ugly, pale and toothless! Instead of those pleasant eyes—pleasant despite a certain unsettling anxiety in them— she should have had sinister orbs looking at you through narrow slits; and her expression, while watching Ben approach, should have been suspicious or crafty. On the contrary, it possessed an almost friendly quality in it, and friendliness was the last thing Ben expected to find at the Black Swan.

The inn was on the right-hand side of the road. Beyond it, on the same side, were one or two other dark, low buildings, showing dim lights that marked their considerable distance from each other. There were no houses on the left. Only blackness that might be anything. If this comprised the whole of Muirgissie, it was a mere tiny village.

'Evenin', miss,' said Ben, as he reached the girl.

'Good evenin',' she answered. She had a nice, rather rich voice, with a pleasant Scotch accent.

'This is the Black Swan, ain't it?'

'Ay.'

'Muirgissie.'

'Ay. The Black Swan, Muirgissie.'

'Boss in?'

'That's my uncle, but he's no hame. Will ye come in and wait? I'm thinkin' he'll no be long.'

She smiled at him. It was the first direct smile he had received for many days. The simplicity of it almost overwhelmed him.

'That's very kind of yer,' said Ben. 'I could do with a sit dahn.'

She smiled again. His accent was as odd to her as hers was to him. Turning, she shoved the front door wide, and he followed her into a large hall. On a wall was a stag's head. Over a door was a glass case containing an enormous stuffed fish. A fishing-rod was in a corner.

'I see yer ketch tiddlers 'ere,' remarked Ben.

The remark beat her, and she opened the door under the stag's head. He entered a parlour full of solid comfort. She waved to a chair, and as he sat down stood before him, making no attempt to hide her curiosity. But it was kindly curiosity.

'Have ye walked far?' she asked.

Unconsciously she put the first awkward question. How far had he walked? Two miles or twenty? Or two hundred? He'd got to be careful! From now onwards, everybody he spoke to was a potential witness in a murder trial.

'I ain't no good at countin',' he answered.

'Ower the moor?'

He thought it best not to deny that. He could have come from the moor without having seen Mr Smith's body.

'That's right, miss.'

'Wha' from?'

'Eh? Well, that's easy, ain't it?'

'I'm gey fond o' guessin', but I'm no clever at it.'

'Gey 'oo?'

'What?'

'I'm sorry, miss, but yer tork so funny—well, that's bein' 'ere, o' course—I can't unnerstand orl yer say.'

'I've aye a notion that you talk funny yoursel',' she retorted, and suddenly threw back her head and laughed.

Ben stared at her. Then he laughed, too. Might as well. It made a change.

'You're no thinkin' me unkind,' she exclaimed, abruptly sobering.

'Lumme, no!' he answered. 'I shouldn't think yer could be unkind ter nobody.'

She looked surprised. 'What makes you say that?'

'Well, see, I can judge fices.'

'Maybe I can, too.' She paused, then added after a moment of hesitation, 'Ay, and see whaur there's trouble!'

''Oo's in trouble?' said Ben anxiously.

'I've no said anyone's in trouble,' she replied. 'Will I light the fire? It's a cold nicht, I'm thinkin'.'

She ran out of the room for a moment, and returned with matches. It certainly did seem a little cold. This crisp mountain air was very different from the stuffy atmosphere of the London flat. Took a bit of getting used to. And a wind had started blowing outside, too, with a doleful sound that added to the sense of chill. He watched her as she stooped and applied the match to the already laid paper and wood. In a few moments there was a crackling blaze. 'Wunnerful wot a bit o' warm can do jest when yer want it,' thought Ben. But he was not referring to the blaze.

'Now will you be answerin' me,' said the girl, as she straightened up again.

'Wot? Ain't I?' replied Ben.

'I was speerin' at you whaur you've come from?'

'So yer was, if that means wot I tike it ter mean. That's right. We're back at the berginnin' agine. But didn't I tell yer?'

'You said it was easy, and I said I was no clever at guessin',' she reminded him.

'Lumme, you don't need no Pellimanism, the way you remember! Well, so it is easy. If I was ter meet you in England I'd say, "She comes from Scotland," by the way yer tork, see, so if you meet me in Scotland you orter say, "'E comes from England," by the way *I* tork, that's right, ain't it?'

She smiled, and shook her head.

'England's a big place! Well, are you tellin' me why you're here, or may I no ken that before my uncle is hame?'

'Corse, I carn't mike yer out,' answered Ben. 'Not that I mind yer questions, nacherly—seein' I know yer ain't arskin' ter trip me up, like some people would—besides, 'oo said there was anythink ter trip me up abart, any'ow?— but, well, miss, this is an inn, ain't it?'

She nodded.

'And if a bloke drops inter an inn, well, that's orl in order, ain't it? 'E wants a drink or a bed, don't 'e?'

She nodded again.

'Well, then, where's the puzzle?'

'You havna asked for a drink or a bed,' she answered.

'Eh?'

'You havna asked for a drink or a bed.'

'Oh! I'm waitin' fer the boss, ain't I?'

'You dinna think you can ask me?'

'Oh!'

Smart, she was! Or was he just a mug? Bit o' both, p'r'aps. But his head was numb like. What with being up all night, and never knowing where he was or who he was, and talking to dead men, and then bumping all of a sudden into a girl like this—it made you a bit silly . . . And the warmth, too . . . What he'd really like would be to take her to the pictures—you know, give her a good time—and go to sleep while she sat in the next seat and enjoyed herself. And then bring her back, p'r'aps, and treat her to a bite of supper—cheese, smoked salmon, anything she liked—and then go to sleep again in this comfortable chair by this warm fire while she ate it . . . And forget about dead people . . . and forget . . . forget . . . Yes, but it wasn't easy to forget about Mr Smith, of Boston! Out there in the wind! Dead as a door-nail. Waiting for somebody to find him! Who would find him? And who had killed him? Poor bloke, p'r'aps he wasn't so bad. Just thought he'd close his eyes and earn a bit of money, and now his eyes were closed for good. What's this about closed eyes? Somebody's eyes closed? They were open . . . open . . . Eh?

He opened his own eyes, and found the girl bending over him.

'How lang is it since you was in bed?' she asked.

'Go on!' blinked Ben.

'You didna know you was asleep?'

'Wot? Popped orf, did I? We orl do in my fambily. Tikes us sudden. Once my father went ter sleep in the middle of eatin' a bernarner, and when 'e woke up and finished it 'e didn't know 'e'd stopped . . . Oi! Wot's the matter?'

His little story about his father ought to have made her laugh. He knew she could laugh. She was made for it. But, instead, she looked worried.

'Will you no tell me why you've come to see my uncle?' she asked, with the first note of pleading in her voice.

It was a new voice. It fitted her expression before she had forgotten her own troubles to think of his. And yet—there was something very odd in her atmosphere—she seemed to be thinking of him as well as herself.

'Well—why not?' answered Ben. 'Yus, arter orl, why not?'

It was terribly depressing to have to lie to this girl, yet unless he risked the success of his whole enterprise there was no alternative. What a relief it would have been if he could have confided in just such a person as this!

'I'm out o' work, see?' he explained. 'And I've bin told there's work ter be picked up 'ere.'

'Who told you?' she asked.

'Well, miss, it was like this. One night some of us got torkin' at a pub. "The plice fer jobs is Scotland," ses one. "And the plice in Scotland is Muirgissie," ses another. "Is that a fack?" I ses. "It's a fack," they ses. "Orl right," I ses, and 'ere I am.'

She regarded him doubtfully as she replied, 'I'm feared you've been gi'en bad advice.'

'Oh!'

'I've no heard o' any work near here.'

'That's a pity.'

'What made you ask for my uncle?'

'I thort 'e'd know if any work was goin'. Or, p'r'aps—'
He paused, and watched her covertly. 'Or, p'r'aps, 'e might
'ave a job for me 'isself?'

She removed her eyes from his face for a moment or
two and stared into the fire. He could see she was thinking
hard. He watched her lips suddenly press together. 'She's
mide up 'er mind ter somethink,' he reflected, 'and it ain't
goin' ter do me any good!'

'What's your name?' she asked, turning back to him.

'Charlie Wilkins,' he answered.

She had evidently not heard the name before, because
she ran on:

'Would you tak' some advice, Mr Wilkins?'

'Well, that derpends on wot it is, don't it?'

'Ay, but it's guid advice. Mr MacTavish—that's my
uncle—he'll not have any work for you.'

'Doncher think so?'

'I ken he wilna. And—and he's got the temper on him
that's no safe.'

'I'm much obliged fer the warnin', miss, but I can look
arter meself.'

'Ay, but you havna met Mr MacTavish!'

'But 'e won't go fer me afore I open me marth, will 'e?
And orl I'm goin' ter arsk 'im is if 'e knows of a job.'

She frowned, and suddenly came closer.

'Mr Wilkins,' she said earnestly. 'I said you hadna met
Mr MacTavish.'

'That's right. Yer did.'

'But *you* havna said you dinna ken him.'

'Eh?'

'Do you?'

'Wot? Ken 'im?' Ben stared. 'Lumme, wot's got yer, miss? I've never met 'im in me life!'

'That's the truth?'

'Nah, git this,' said Ben. 'If Mr MacTavish, wot I never knew 'is nime even till yer told me jest nah—if 'e was ter walk inter this 'ere room, I wouldn't know it was 'im, strike me purple, I wouldn't! There, that sounds good enough, don't it?'

She looked relieved.

'Wot mide yer arsk?' he inquired, glad that on this occasion, at least, he had been able to avoid a lie.

'I believe—he's expecting someone,' she replied, hesitating.

'Oh! Do yer?' murmured Ben. He took out his handkerchief and dabbed his forehead. 'Bit ot' like, ain't it? Did 'e tell yer 'e was?'

'No.'

'And yer—yer don't know 'is nime, or nothink?'

She shook her head.

'Then 'ow—'

'We won't mind about that. But as you're not the man my uncle's expectin', I'm thinkin' it will be best for you to go. I'm sorry, it's a sair pity, but I'm speakin' for your guid.'

Ben answered her, after a short pause. 'There's one thing, miss, I carn't mike out. If yer think yer uncle's expeckin' some 'un, though proberly yer on'y think it 'cos yer want a 'oller-day livin' in this, well, gloomy sort o' plice, well, it is, ain't it, though mind yer why shouldn't 'e expeck some 'un—where am I, oh, yus. If wot I sed, why didn't yer think I was the bloke right from the start, see? Or did yer?'

'No, I didna think it was you at the start,' she responded, when she had sorted the question out.

'Why not?'

'I was guessin' you wouldna be that sort o' man.'

'Wot, a wrong 'un?'

'Maybe ay, and maybe no.'

'Orl right. But yer chinged yer mind. Fust I wasn't, then p'r'aps I was. Eh?' She nodded. 'Wot 'appened ter mike yer chinge yer mind?'

'Do you ken you talk in your sleep, Mr Wilkins?'

'Gawd! I mean, lumme!'

'You said something when you were asleep just now.'

'Wot was it?'

'I only heard four words.'

'Let's 'ave 'em?'

'"Dead as a door-nail."'

'Go on!'

'And then, when I woke you up, Havers, how you jumped!'

Ben swallowed, then grinned.

'Corse I jumped, miss! I was dead as a doornail, wasn't I? And I expeck I was jest menshuning the fack when yer brought me ter life agine!' He squinted at her, to see how she was taking it. 'Me father torked in 'is sleep, too. That time I told yer abart—"Cut 'im in two," 'e ses. But, corse, 'e on'y meant the bernarner.'

He missed the little glow of pride and satisfaction that ought to have accompanied this nimble lying. The girl's eyes were too grave and honest.

'I am sure you are not ane to do wrong,' she answered, 'and that's why I'm no wantin' you to get in trouble.'

'Well, there's more'n one sort o' trouble,' he replied, 'and I'll tell yer one kind I ain't keen on.' He glanced towards the red-curtained window. ''Ark ter the wind! If I go, where am I goin' ter? I don't fancy wanderin' abart orl night!' The wind rose suddenly to a high moan through which some other sound percolated. As the wind decreased, the other sound grew louder, taking its place. It was a car.

''Allo—is that yer uncle?'

'No,' said the girl, now turning her eyes also towards the window. 'He's walkin'.'

They waited in silence for the car to pass. Its pace slackened, and it stopped.

''Nother visiter?' inquired Ben.

The girl did not move. Again they waited in silence, this time for a ring or a knock. Again, the expected did not happen.

'P'r'aps they rung and we didn't 'ear,' suggested Ben, uneasily.

Why did he feel so uneasy? Nothing in a motorcar stopping outside an inn, was there? But the girl seemed to share his uneasiness, and all at once, with her eyes still fixed on the window, she raised her hands convulsively and clasped them. An eye had appeared in the little narrow space between the edge of the red curtain and the window-frame.

It was there only for an instant. As quickly as it had appeared, it vanished.

'Lumme, wot was that?' gasped Ben.

He lurched from his chair and ran to the window. He pulled the curtain aside as the car started to move again.

He saw the back of the car just before it slipped out of the small patch of light cast by the now uncurtained window. He let the curtain go, his brain spinning.

It was the Ford which, when he had last seen it, had contained the dead body of Mr Smith.

A few moments later the front door slammed. Heavy footsteps sounded in the hall. The parlour door was opened, and a tall, sandy-haired man walked in.

12

MacTavish

Ben's impression that this must be MacTavish, the inn-keeper, was confirmed by the newcomer's opening words.

'Ah, Jean!' he exclaimed. 'Anybody come?'

Then he noticed Ben, and his sandy, protruding eyebrows went up. The eyebrows were thickly tangled, and had never heard of a comb.

'Evenin', sir,' murmured Ben.

Ben's brain was still spinning, but all one could do was to carry on and to see where the spinning led.

'He's called after work,' explained Jean, quickly, 'but I was tellin' him—'

'Weel, I'll do the tellin',' interrupted her uncle brusquely. 'Go awa' and do some work. No, bide a wee. There was a car.'

'Ay,' answered Jean, frowning.

'It stoppit. Was he in it?' He jerked his head towards Ben.

'He wasna.'

'Weel, lass, weel! Wha was in it?'

'I dinna ken.'

'Dinna ken?'

'You haird me.'

'I haird ye, I haird ye fine, but now you can be hearin' me! The car stoppit, I'm tellin' ye, I saw it up the road, and somebody got out.'

He looked at her suspiciously, and she flushed with sudden anger.

'Ay, somebody got out,' she retorted, 'and somebody looked in the window, and somebody got in again, and somebody drove awa'. And now somebody's gaen back to her work, and you can get on wi' your secrets wi' Mr Wilkins!'

Whereupon she turned on her attractive heel and stormed out of the room.

Ben stared after her, but MacTavish was staring at Ben. All at once Ben became conscious of it.

'Was Wilkins the name?' inquired MacTavish softly.

'Yus, that's me,' replied Ben.

The innkeeper walked to the door, peered out into the hall, and closed the door.

'Weel, Mr Wilkins,' he said, 'and wha may you hae come to Muirgissie aboot?'

'Oh! Yer dunno, eh?'

'I ken wha I'm told.'

'I see. Well, *she* tole yer.'

'Oh, ay. You're lookin' for a wee bit worrk?'

'That's right.'

'But wha brocht ye to Muirgissie?'

'Well, I 'eard there was some goin', see?'

'Ah, ye haird?'

'Yus, I 'aird.'

'And wha tole ye?'

'Wot?'

'Dinna I speak plain?'

'Yus, but I on'y unnerstand English. 'Oo told me, eh? Well, you know 'ow these things git abart. It was jest people torkin', if yer know wot I mean.'

'Maybe I know fine what you mean, Mr Wilkins. And maybe I respect your caution. We'll say nae mair aboot that, juist for the moment. But will you be tellin' me whit kind o' worrk you hae in mind?'

'I ain't pertickler.'

'No?'

'When I tike on a job, I jest does wot I'm told,' said Ben, watching the innkeeper as closely as the innkeeper was watching him.

'Weel, that's as it should be,' agreed MacTavish, nodding his large, untidy head. 'When a man taks on a job, he taks it on.' The logic appeared unassailable. 'But I'm no sayin' I can gie you the job,' he added quickly. 'We're juist— probin'. Ay, probin'. To see how the land lies. Why, 'tis easy to talk, but there's a differ between talkin' and doin', ay, and between weel-doin' and ill-doin'.' He stared into the fire. 'Tak' this example. By your talk, your name is Wilkins.'

He paused. The probing was a slow, laborious business. He turned from the fire, and fixed his eyes on Ben again. He had two teeth missing, and the economy which had refused substitutes had not assisted his personal appearance.

'That's right,' said Ben. 'C. Wilkins. C fer Charles.'

'Ay, but wha's the proof?'

'Well, I ain't brort me birth certificate.'

'Then you canna prove—'

'Yus, I can! 'Arf a mo'!' He dived into his pocket, and produced the visiting card given to him by Mr Smith, of Boston. ''Ow abart that?'

MacTavish took the card and regarded it closely. Then he handed it back.

'Thank you, Mr Wilkins,' he said. 'You'll be stayin' the nicht, I'm thinkin', but there's mair to ken yet. How did ye come?'

'Eh?'

'Was it alane?'

'No.'

'No?' MacTavish frowned. 'Wha was wi' ye?'

'Eh?'

'You're gey fond o' that worrd!' exclaimed the innkeeper, his frown increasing. 'Wha was wi' ye, mon, wha was wi' ye?'

'Well, I carn't unnerstan' yer if I carn't unnerstan' yer, carn't I?' retorted Ben.

'Nobody was with me.'

MacTavish cast his eyes towards the ceiling.

'Naebody was wi' ye—'

'No—'

'But when I ask how ye came you said it wasna alane!'

'That's right, I came over the moor.'

'The moor? Wha' hae the moor to do wi't?'

'It wasn't a lane. Leastwise, not afore I was leavin' the moor, see? Then I come dahn a lane. Now 'ave we got it?'

MacTavish crossed to a small cupboard on the wall and took out a pipe. He seemed to need soothing. Then he drew a deep breath, and began again.

'You walked into Muirgissie by yersel'?'

'Yus. Ay. That's right,' agreed Ben.

'And when you say that, you're meanin' that naebody was wi' ye?'

'If you mean wot I mean, then that's wot I mean. Corse, I might 'ave got a bit of a lift part o' the way, but that wouldn't 'urt, would it? Och, ay?'

The innkeeper let the question go while he filled his pipe and lit it. He had momentarily lost his power to concentrate. Then, after a few consoling and mind-clearing puffs, he proceeded:

'Now, leesten, Mr Wilkins. We maun bide a wee to comprehend the language o' the other and learn the differ, but I hae a notion we can get along fine and needna wait if we dinna fash oursel's.'

'I can fash any dinner yer put afore me in a couple o' ticks,' answered Ben.

The innkeeper let this go, also.

'There's ane mair question,' he went on, doggedly, 'and it's aboot that car. My niece, you haird her, she said that somebody got out o' the car and looked in at the window. Was that the truth?'

'Yus.'

'Did you see wha it was?'

'No. It was gorn too quick.'

'But you can say if it was—a woman?'

'Couldn't say if it was a snike! See, orl I spotted was the eyes, and when yer don't spot wot's rahnd 'em, yer done. They jest looked in and 'opped it.'

MacTavish glanced towards the window as though attempting to recreate the vision, but the red curtains refused to oblige. In the little silence that followed it was obvious that MacTavish was worried.

101

'Well—'ave I got the job?' inquired Ben, breaking the silence.

'Job?' repeated the innkeeper, vaguely. He turned from the window. His expression was moody. 'Maybe—I'll want you for it in the mornin'.'

'Mebbe,' thought Ben, 'the pleece'll want me fust fer somethink else! Do they 'ang yer in Scotland, sime as England? Or is it that eleckertrooshen?'

13

And so to Bed

Then MacTavish left the room. His heavy footsteps receded across the hall.

In a few minutes Jean returned, with a cloth over her arm. Her manner was composed, but by will-power rather than instinct, and beneath her deliberate movements there was a nervous tension. She had smoothed her gold hair—it was the gold of nature, not of the shop, and had merely slipped out of light brown—and Ben wondered vaguely why she had bothered. It couldn't have been for him that she had patted disobedient curls into place; or for her uncle, whose personal example stood for tangle. It did not cross Ben's mind that she might have done it for herself.

'So you're stayin' the nicht,' she observed, as she drew a small table near the fire and spread the cloth over it.

'That's right,' answered Ben. 'And the on'y one 'oo is, by the look of it.'

'Ay, there's naebody else,' she replied.

Something in her tone caught Ben's attention. Was it an underlying weariness against which her brightness warred—or had she been crying since he had last seen her? There was a suspicious heaviness around her eyes, and the extra touch of tidiness might have been part of a necessary process to conceal some new distress.

'Then there won't be no dancin' 'ere ternight,' remarked Ben.

A look of surprise was followed by a smile.

'We dinna dance in Muirgissie,' she said.

'That's a pity,' he commented. 'I like a bit of a 'op, yer know—watchin'. I carn't do it meself, I falls over.'

'Maybe you wouldna if you had some teachin'.'

'It wouldn't mike no differ. Dif'rence. Lumme, I'm catchin' it! I 'ad a dancin' lesson once, but it laid us both up for a fortnight!'

Jean laughed. It was the first time he had heard her laughter, and it transformed the room for an instant. The instant was short-lived, however, for she relapsed abruptly into solemnity as though she had been guilty of joking at a funeral.

'Did my uncle tell you wha you could get some work?' she inquired.

''E ses 'e might 'ave somethink fer me termorrer,' responded Ben.

'What! Himsel'?' she exclaimed, startled.

'Well—p'r'aps I didn't unnerstan' 'im quite correck,' he answered, wondering whether he could ever engineer a complete conversation without putting his foot in it somewhere. 'See, some o' these Scotch words tike a bit o' learnin'.'

On the point of leaving the room she paused to look at him rather suspiciously.

'My uncle wasna as cross wi' you as I expeckit.'

'Corse 'e wasn't,' Ben replied to the almost challenging statement. 'Why should 'e?'

'He's in a bad humour with every one.'

'Yus, but I ain't hevery one, and it tikes two ter mike a quarrel.'

'My uncle can quarrel for baith!'

'Not when I'm one o' the baith! People don't quarrel with me, miss—they jest 'its me or leaves me.'

She gave an odd little sigh, and departed.

'She ain't sure o' me yet,' reflected Ben. 'Becorse 'er uncle didn't kick me aht, she thinks I'm the bloke wot 'e's expeckin'—yus, and I am!'

For a moment he thought he really was, till he suddenly recollected that he wasn't.

In a short while Jean returned, bringing a plate packed with meat, greens, and potatoes. Momentarily life took on a rosier hue as she placed the plate before him.

'Where are you 'avin' your'n?' he inquired.

'In the kitchen wi' uncle,' she answered.

'The kitching would 'ave done fer me.'

'He prefaired you to hae it here.'

'Oh! I see,' said Ben. 'And wot 'appens arterwards? When I've done?'

'If you're tired as I'm thinkin' you are,' she replied, 'you'll be wantin' your bed.'

He was tired, and physically ready for bed, but he did not want to be sent there.

'We ain't goin' ter 'ave a 'ob-nob, then?' he asked.

'I'll be finishin' me work,' she said, after a moment's hesitation. 'We've nae servant.'

'Wot—jest you and yer uncle?'

'Ay.'

'Yer kep' at it, ain't yer?'

'There's aye muckle to do.'

'Well, see, could I lend a 'and with the muckle? You could show me 'ow?'

Her lip trembled for a moment, and then, as though the situation were beyond her, she shook her head, turned abruptly, and left him alone again.

It was disappointing.

But disappointment did not spoil his appetite, and he had reduced the plate to its pattern long before a second plate was brought to him. The second plate contained apple pudding, and the bearer this time was the innkeeper himself.

Ben noticed at once that MacTavish's demeanour had undergone a subtle change. It was less guarded, more friendly. The eye that gleamed blackly beneath its tangled eyebrow had lost most of its suspicion and antagonism, and in their place was a suggestion of dry, secretive humour. 'We're getting to understand each other,' his attitude hinted, 'though, of course, we're still being careful!'

'Weel, Mr Wilkins,' he observed, as he regarded Ben's work on the first course, 'You're no doin' so bad!'

'When it comes ter puttin' food away,' replied Ben, 'I'll play anybody.'

'Nae doot. But I hope you recognise, Mr Wilkins, that you're receivin' quality as weel as quantity.'

'I reckernise that,' nodded Ben. 'And p'r'aps there's somethink I orter reckernise, too, afore we gits much further.'

MacTavish looked a little surprised, and dropped his voice.

'You'll mention it the noo?' he murmured.

'Why not?'

'Maybe there's nae reason at all why not,' responded the innkeeper.

'See, I b'leeve in knowin' where yer stand—speshully when it's ter do with fernance.' He winked. 'Wot's goin' ter be the damage?'

Now MacTavish looked more surprised, and glanced towards the door.

'You'll not be expectin' me to name that?' he exclaimed.

'Oh!' said Ben. Had he put his foot in it again? Perhaps Scottish innkeepers were sensitive about their bills. 'Leave it ter the mornin', eh?'

'Ay,' frowned MacTavish. ''Tis nowt you'll be gettin' frae me!'

The atmosphere became a little less comfortable. Failing to find the reason, Ben gave up, and fell back upon the more understandable operation of eating. The innkeeper watched him glumly, as though he were reckoning the cost of each mouthful.

'You'll be goin' to bed when you've finished?' inquired MacTavish heavily.

'I dunno,' answered Ben. Everybody wanted to send him to bed! Or didn't they? Maybe he was reading significance into the most ordinary remarks. If a cat had come in and scratched itself, he would have regarded it with suspicion. 'P'r'aps I'll stay up fer a bit.'

'You'll nae be goin' oot?'

'Matter if I did?'

'Weel—we lock up early here, ye ken.'

Ben shrugged his shoulders. After all, he didn't want to go out. He might meet unpleasant things in the wind that was moaning around Muirgissie! So why worry to argue?

'That's O.K. with me,' he said. 'I ain't goin' ter the pickchers.'

As though to ensure that he did not escape, MacTavish remained in the room while Ben demolished the apple pudding, wandering about vaguely and pretending to do things. When the plate was empty he pounced upon it and carted it to the kitchen. He was back again in a few seconds, a candle in his hand.

'I'll be showin' ye your room,' he announced.

The hall, with its stuffed fish and stags' heads and general atmosphere of preserved dead, had been gloomy enough when Ben had first entered it, but it seemed doubly gloomy now that MacTavish was substituted for his niece and the light of a flickering candle created fantastic shadows. As they left the parlour, the antlers immediately over the door were momentarily repeated in exaggerated blackness on the ceiling. It was as though their dark soul had escaped for an instant, to slide back the next moment into the static source from which they had leapt. At the top of the staircase were more antlers, from which shot more momentarily moving shadows. 'Tork abart black spiders!' thought Ben.

Queer idea of decoration some people had! Animals' heads and fishes' bodies. If you had to put things on your walls, why not pictures of Shirley Temple?

And why, too, this candlelight?

'Savin' helectricity?' inquired Ben, as they reached the top of the staircase and began moving along another unlit hall.

'There's nae electreecity here to save,' answered the innkeeper, 'but if there was I'd be savin' it after bedtime.'

'Oh, it's arter bedtime, is it?'

'Ay, fer them as rises airly.'

'Oh! But s'pose some 'un comes along as wants a room fer the night.'

'They'll be ringin', I reckon.'

'Not if they don't see no light. They'll go by the 'otel and miss it!'

'You dinna miss whit you dinna ken,' answered MacTavish, 'and as I wouldna ken they had missed the Black Swan, the Black Swan wouldna miss them.'

He opened a door, thrust his hairy hand in, and deposited the candle on a stool just inside.

'Guid-nicht, Mr Wilkins,' he said. 'You'll be called i' the mornin'.'

'Yes, and we'll finish our chat in the mornin',' added Ben.

'Ay,' nodded MacTavish. 'Ay.' Suddenly his manner changed again, and there was a return of the friendliness that had evinced itself in the parlour for a few moments. 'This is a delicate business, Mr Wilkins, there's nae need to remind you,' he said, 'and it's my dooty to be cautious. We're no wantin' a repetition of wha' happened the first time, ye ken.' He lowered his voice in lugubrious reminiscence. 'Losh, no! So if mebbe I hae been a wee bit short wi' you, you'll tak' it in an understandin' speerit?'

''Oo's complainin'?' answered Ben, wondering anxiously what calamity had happened the first time, and whether there existed any means by which he could find out, to avoid the undesired repetition.

'That's a' recht,' muttered MacTavish, 'that's a' recht,' and turned to go. But something still seemed to be bothering him. Pausing in the doorway, he suddenly said, 'That face at the window, Mr Wilkins—I wunner—are you sure you canna bring it to mind, now? Are you sure you canna say if it was a woman?'

'I couldn't say if it was a cat,' replied Ben.

'Weel, there's some haud there's nae differ,' observed MacTavish, as the candlelight flickered on the wraith of a smile. 'Which reminds me of ane mair thing.' The smile vanished, and the innkeeper's features became heavy again. 'It's aboot my niece. It will be juist as weel if you do not get too conversational wi' her. Though, after all,' he added, 'I'm thinkin' there wull be nae sic danger o' that.'

The next moment he was gone, and Ben listened to his footsteps as they grew fainter and fainter along the dark passage.

14

By Candlelight

Sleep, though needed, was impossible. In the flickering candlelight, Ben sat and thought.

His brain was groping in a region of thick black clouds, and the thickness and the blackness increased the farther he advanced into them. Would he ever be able to grope his way out again, if he wanted to? And did he want to? He could not find a definite answer to either question.

At first the issue had been a fairly simple one. He had seen a detective killed, and he had decided to carry on for him. All he had to do was to go back to a woman's flat and discover a secret. He would tell the secret to Scotland Yard, and the woman, with her accomplices, would be arrested.

But the woman had not revealed her secret. At the bidding of some new personality (designated, for convenience, as the Jack of Clubs), she had sent Ben on a second journey to a mysterious cottage in Lincolnshire, where he had passed into the temporary keeping of Mr Smith, of Boston. In his turn, Mr Smith had passed him on to Scotland, where he was now residing at a mysterious hotel in charge of Mr MacTavish of Muirgissie.

A traveller of importance wherever he called, he was a traveller without knowledge. He received none, and was as far from solving the puzzle as he had been at the beginning.

Was the Black Swan to be journey's end, or would the journey continue beyond it—up into the mountains that reared their invisible heads far out in the blackness beyond his window? Would the final instructions come from the dour Scotsman, or would MacTavish pass him on once more to somebody else? 'Blimy if I ain't like a paiper packet,' thought Ben, 'bein' 'anded abart, and the larst person wot 'as it opens it and gits the surprise!'

But the unsolved mystery was not the sole cause of Ben's increasing complexity. Two new personalities had entered into the maze to worry him since he had stood on the bridge—at the entrance to the maze—with the detective.

One was the innkeeper's niece, Jean. What was a nice, bright young girl like her doing in this gloomy hole, having her gaiety ground out by the thumb of a scamp? For it was as obvious that MacTavish was a scamp as it was that Jean was a nice bright girl. 'She *orter* be dancin','' decided Ben, recalling their conversation, 'instead o' bein' sent ter bed at nursery-time arter workin' without no skivvy. Yus, and I'd like ter sit and watch 'er!' The knight in him stirred towards his grubby surface, desiring with the splendid illogicality of knights to effect a rescue. He wanted to carry Jean into a world of sunlight—forgetting that he, like Jean herself, was more accustomed to the shadows.

The other person who worried him—more strangely, but at the moment more persistently—was Mr Smith, of Boston. In life Ben had not cared for Mr Smith. In death, he thought of him with a queer compassion. If he had been a link in a chain of doubtful quality—and, obviously, he had been—he had not apparently represented a major link. For some reward he would never now be able to enjoy, he had undertaken to convey Ben from one point to another, knowing as little as he could, and closing his eyes tightly lest he should learn more.

'P'r'aps 'e was poor and kep' 'is old mother,' thought Ben, excusing him lavishly, 'and p'r'aps 'e wanted the money fer medereine . . . Funny 'ow much more yer like a bloke arter 'e's dead!'

An appalling idea hit him in the stomach. It hit him so hard that it brought him to his feet and nearly sent the candle over. He'd taken Mr Smith for dead. Suppose—he wasn't?

But as Ben recalled the gruesome vision he had watched being blotted out by the night, he felt certain that Mr Smith, of Boston had breathed his last, and that it was not he who had driven by the hotel and peered into the parlour. The person who had done that was the person who knew, even more certainly than Ben himself, that Mr Smith was dead.

Where was that person now? Ben turned to the dark view outside his bedroom window, and the question slid in like a cold draught. Or like a chilly hand the fingers of which were trying to draw him out. Other questions glided in through the undecipherable darkness. Why had MacTavish thought it might be a woman? Why had he been so anxious that it was not a woman? What woman? . . . *Had* it been a woman? . . . What had gone wrong the first time? . . . What first time? . . . Where was Mr Smith now?

'Corse, I can't stand much more o' this!' pondered Ben. 'I gotter find out—'

113

Someone knocked softly on the door behind him. He swung round quickly.

"Oo's that?' he whispered.

Then, annoyed with himself for having whispered—he had a right to his voice, hadn't he?—he asked loudly:

"Oo's that?'

His voice now seemed to boom.

There was no reply. The knock had not been repeated. He opened the door and stared out into the empty darkness. No, the darkness was not quite empty a little way along the passage. Something was flitting away.

'Am I frightened?' he asked himself, as he ran out after it. 'Yus!'

So, apparently, was the ghost he was chasing. When he caught hold of it (for he could race any ghost, coming or going), it tottered, and nearly fell back into his arms. It was Jean, in her dressing-gown.

'Wozzer matter?' whispered Ben.

He did not correct the whisper this time. It was too appropriate to the occasion.

'Nothing,' the girl whispered back.

'Was it you wot knocked?'

'Ay.'

She released herself from his grip and turned to face him. He could just see her outline. He noticed that her hair was no longer neat and trim.

'Well—I answered yer,' said Ben.

'I haird you,' she replied.

'Oh! Then why didn't yer answer back?'

'I—I juist wanted to ken you were in your room.'

'Well, I were.'

'Ay.'

114

'Wot mide yer think I mightn't be?'

She hesitated, then hedged.

'If you hadna been, I couldna hae locked up.'

'I see. And nah yer goin' ter, miss? In yer nightdress?'

She did not reply, and he knew the reason. She was not going to lock up. Either she or her uncle had already done so.

'We canna stand talkin' here?' she whispered suddenly, darting a glance along the passage.

Again Ben knew the reason. They were not supposed to be talking at all. Her uncle had warned Ben, and had probably given instructions to Jean, also. But why shouldn't they talk if they wanted to? Perhaps there were things that *ought* to be talked about!

'Would yer step inter my room fer a minit?' asked Ben. 'It's orl right, I ain't gorn ter bed yet.'

The superfluous information was intended for the invisible Mrs Grundy. Mrs Grundy might have retorted that Jean had obviously gorn to bed, and had got up again, but the Guardian of Proprieties was not really interested in scarecrows like Ben, who could not produce the compliment of her suspicion.

Once more Jean hedged.

'Why have you no' gone to bed?' she inquired.

'That's wot I wanter tell yer,' answered Ben, hoping to clinch her curiosity.

He began to move back to his room. She followed him. A few seconds later they were in the bedroom, looking at each other by candlelight.

'Nah, then,' said Ben, closing the door, 'wot was the real reason yer knocked?'

'I told you,' she replied.

'Ter find aht if I was in, yus, but you ain't told me why you wanted ter find aht.'

'I told you that, too.'

'Oh! Well, miss—not meanin' ter be rude like—would yer try agine?'

'That sounds very rude!'

'On'y becorse yer carn't judge me by the sound. See, I ain't got the 'ang o' perlite words.'

A look of despair shot into her face.

'It's nae use, I canna mak you out!' she exclaimed, almost angrily. 'Ilka time I'm thinkin' ane way, you're up sayin' something that mak's me think the other!' She suddenly seized his shoulders. Her fingers were strong, but trembling. 'Who are you? Wha hae you come from, and wha' are you doin' here in Muirgissie?'

She stared at him hard, as though trying to pierce his eyes to the mind behind. Then, as suddenly as she had taken hold of him, she whipped her hands away again and turned her head towards the door. Ben was no artist, and his physical reactions (saving the unpleasant ones) had become dulled through lack of use, but even at that tense moment when he began to grow as interested in the window as she was in the door, he was conscious of the line of her turned neck making a graceful, candle-lit contour against the gloomy background of the wall. It affected him queerly, reviving with almost painful force his incoherent desire to be of some assistance to her.

'Got an idea,' he muttered, trying to think of one.

She turned swiftly.

'Wot abart sittin' dahn?'

'Was that the idea?' she asked, as he shoved a chair towards her. But she sat down, and watched him curiously while he moved slowly towards the window. Just before he reached it she spoke again, this time rather sharply.

'Be careful!'

He stopped at once. Whether the chair had been the idea or not, he was now getting another.

'You 'eard somethink aht there?' he asked.

She nodded. So, now, did he.

'Was that wot got yer up?'

She nodded again.

'Was that why yer come 'ere, ter me?'

'Weel—I wanted to be sure it wasna you.'

'I see. Well, it ain't, so wot abart lettin' yer uncle know?'

After a little pause she said, 'He isna in his room.'

'Oh! Yer know that?'

'Ay.'

'Bin there, eh? And then come along ter me. Well, miss, as I'm in and 'e ain't, it's proberly 'im, ain't it?'

She was silent, and he gained an impression that for some reason she did not think the person outside was her uncle.

'Look 'ere, s'pose I 'adn't bin 'ere, wot would you 'ave done?' he asked. 'And why did yer run away like that when yer fahnd I *was* 'ere?'

'And why should I be answerin' all your questions when you'll no be answerin' mine?' she retorted suddenly.

'That's right,' agreed Ben, nodding. 'Yer want fifty-fifty. Well, 'oo wouldn't? I ain't blamin' yer.'

All at once he completed his journey to the window and peered out. A gleam of light vanished abruptly. A large black bush waved violently, and then became still.

He left the window, and returned to the girl. She was on her feet again.

117

'Yus, there's some 'un aht there,' he said. 'Like me ter go aht and see if it's yer uncle?'

'But—suppose it isna?' she answered.

'Then p'r'aps it wouldn't be so nice,' he admitted.

'But you'd go?'

'If yer wanted it, miss.'

'You'd do it—for me?'

'Corse I would!'

'Why?'

'Well, miss—yer dunno why, do yer? Wot I mean is, yer jest do or yer don't, ain't it?'

'You're the queerest mon I ever met, Mr Wilkins,' she said, with puzzled earnestness. 'If it wasna for—' She broke off, and shook her head. 'You'll gang oot yon for me, and maybe be gi'en a broken head, but you willna answer my questions—so wha' must I be thinkin'?'

'Lumme, if I ain't careful she'll beat me!' thought Ben. Aloud he answered, 'The reason I ain't answerin' yer questions is 'cos I carn't, there, that's stright, ain't it?'

'Is it?'

'Orl right. 'Ere's somethink strighter. I carn't answer yer questions 'cos I carn't, but I'll answer one yer ain't arsked. It's abart you, and this is wot it is. None o' the questions wot I carn't answer would 'urt you if I could answer 'em, or if they would, they ain't goin' ter, there, 'ow abart that?'

She stepped closer to him, and her hand touched the lapel of his coat. She withdrew it with a little cry.

'Wozzat?' he asked.

He lifted the lapel, to find out what had caused the trouble, and as he did so the little skull-pin grinned up at them.

She stared at it for a few moments in horror. Then, as a door slammed somewhere below, she turned and fled.

15

Friend in Need

Moments come when there are so many things to do that you adopt the alternative of doing nothing. Such a moment now came to Ben.

He could have followed Jean, overtaken her again, and attempted to explain the skull-pin. He could have descended to the spot below from which the door had slammed. He could have returned to the window and gazed at the large dark bush, watching for the revelation of its secret. Or, following an earlier impulse which had dawned before Jean had knocked on his door, and from which the knocking had diverted him, he could slip out of the inn (assuming that were still possible) and revisit the spot where he had last seen Mr Smith of Boston. That spot was constantly in his mind. The car, he knew, was no longer there. But was Mr Smith's body there—lying by the lane for anyone to see, or hidden in a ditch? Or wasn't it there?

But instead he obeyed a sudden irresistible impulse to lie down on the bed and see what happened. And what happened was hardly less sudden than the impulse to await it. It was sleep. Nature had stepped in at last, and had decided to call it a day.

He awoke with a start. This was the way he usually awoke, due to a chronic sensation renewed each morning that he had done something wrong, although he could never remember what it was. Actually he lived with the weight of the world upon him, and his greatest sin was in having been born . . . Darkness had vanished. In its place was a queer white light. The light was queer because, somehow or other, it was as suffocating as the darkness had been. Looking towards the window, he saw mist.

He rose from his bed and went to the window. The view was a sea of slowly moving white. It curled and coiled as it moved, assuming strange shapes that formed an endless procession of filmy wraiths travelling through space from nowhere to nowhere. Below he could dimly see the large bush that had once been black. The blackness had gone with its secret. Ahead, somewhere beyond the new white legions, were the invisible mountains with their own secrets—unless these floating forms were themselves the mountains, dissolved and drifting.

There was a washstand in the room. The jug was full of water, a new cake of Pears' soap was in a china dish, and a large clean towel hung over a rail. 'I'll bet it was 'er, not 'im, wot done orl this,' thought Ben, as he began his ablutions. Might as well start the day clean, anyway, when you got the chance.

He wondered what the time was. As he was towelling his face a grandfather clock began wheezing information from the hall below. He stopped and counted. It wheezed up to nine, though the last one was a bit of a struggle.

'Go on!' muttered Ben, in surprise.

Had he slept all that time? He supposed he must have. But it seemed funny. And why hadn't someone given him a knock?

When his meagre toilet was over he stepped out into the passage. Quiet, everything was. There ought to be sounds of cups and things, and the smell of bacon cooking. They couldn't have had breakfast, could they? That would be a dirty trick! Perhaps they had theirs early, and permitted guests to choose their own time!

'Arter orl,' he reflected, as he began to move towards the stairs, 'I s'pose I am a sort o' guest, ain't I? Or ain't I?'

Everything looked horribly white. If it had been snow outside that would have been nice—Ben liked snow, it made you think of silly things like fairies—but he hated mist. That made you think of witches and Chinamen. Ben had never cottoned on to Chinamen since one had tickled him with a knife. The one really bright spot in his present adventure was that, so far, it hadn't included a Chinaman.

A stag's head greeted him at the head of the stairs.

'Merry Christmas,' said Ben.

It was the whiteness that made him think of Christmas, but there was no other resemblance to the festive occasion.

He descended the stairs. As he reached the bottom someone darted at him. It was Jean. She seized his coat and, with surprising strength, lugged him across the hall to the parlour. The window-curtains were not yet drawn, despite the hour, and they stood breathlessly in the half-light. She still held his coat with her right hand while she raised a finger of her left almost to his lips. They were so close he could feel her breath against his face in little warm puffs. He heard her heart, too. Or was it his own?

They stood motionless for what seemed to him an eternity.

Steps sounded from the back of the hall, drawing closer. She had closed the parlour door, and Ben waited for it to open again, combating new terror. 'I wish I was one o' them 'eroes,' he thought, complaining to Fate of the mould in which he had been made. 'This is fair gittin' me!'

There were four feet. Ben specialised in footsteps, and could count the number up to eight. Two were MacTavish's. Whose were the others?

Then the owner of the second pair spoke, his voice sounding immediately outside the door.

'This weather's not goin' to help any.'

Ben did not recognise the voice, but he recognised the innkeeper's:

'Ay, and it's no improvin' any.'

'Well, never fear,' answered the other, 'we'll find him.'

The footsteps had paused.

'Will ye step in for a wee drappie?' asked MacTavish.

Jean's fingers tightened on Ben's sleeve.

'That's very kind of you,' came the reply. 'But I'll have it later.'

The footsteps sounded again. The front door opened and closed. Two figures made two vague smudges on the window-curtain for a moment, then slid off it.

Suddenly Ben found Jean's face even closer to his. Her eyes were so near that they seemed larger than life-size and her lips almost brushed his as they moved, but had they been farther he would not have heard their words, which were scarcely louder than thought.

'Did you do it?' she whispered.

'Do wot?' he whispered back; though he knew what.

'They've found—a dead man!'

Ben swallowed slowly, then answered:

'Yer knows I didn't do it.'

'Whit mak's you think that?'

'Well, yer shoved me in 'ere. Do yer stand fer murder? Nor don't I.'

Her legs suddenly gave way, and she sank into a chair.

'My uncle thinks you did it,' she muttered.

'Oh, does 'e?' murmured Ben. 'Then why didn't 'e let the copper tork ter me? Copper's English fer bobby, in case yer don't know.'

'He didna ken you were in here—he thought you were in your room.'

'Yus, I guessed that, miss, but 'e didn't tike the bobby up ter my room. Why didn't 'e?'

'Shouldn't I be askin' you that?' she replied, shrewdly.

Ben nodded.

'I expeck yer right. Though, corse . . .' He stared at her. 'No, nothink's o' corse! As I ain't tellin' yer nothink, and as yer saw my little, well, ornerment larst night, why don't *you* think I done it, like 'e does?'

'I know a guid mon when I see him,' she answered, 'though I'm fair perplexed.'

'Wot, me good?' exclaimed Ben. 'I don't mean I go abart killin' blokes, I bar that kind o' thing, but—well, any'ow, wot 'appened, see, it's orl come rather sudden.'

'They found him in a lane at the foot o' the moor,' she said, 'early this mornin' it was, before the mist was so thick or they wouldna hae seen him, but they dinna ken wha he is, for he had naething on him—'

'Wot, nikid?'

'Dinna mak me laugh when I'm mair nigh greetin'! He had naething in his pockets, nae letters, nae papers, and the puir mon had been shot—'

Yes, of course he had been shot. That was no news to Ben. But now for the first time he recollected that he had not heard the sound of the shot. And he had not been far off when it had happened . . .

'Well, miss—go on.'

'There's no much mair,' she replied. 'Sergeant Bruce, him you heard just noo, he's been here a'most an hour, pokin' around and speerin' at my uncle. "Has anybody been here?" he asks, and my uncle answers, "Nae, naebody. There's just Jean and mysel," he says, "and naebody else in the hoose," and I knowin' that you're upstairs all the while and prayin' you'll keep sleepin' on so heavy and no' come down.'

'Yus, I was sleepin' 'eavy,' said Ben. 'I s'pose that was why yer didn't wike me?'

'Ay! What would the sergeant be thinkin', after all that lyin'?'

'That's right. And I s'pose *you* 'ad ter lie ter keep yer uncle company like?' She nodded. 'Lumme, wot a tangle! Fust 'e lies thinkin' I done it, and then you lie thinkin' I ain't done it, but not becos' yer think I ain't done it but becos' 'e lied thinkin' I done it without you knowin' why 'e lied! Well, somethink like that, any'ow. Yus—but this is wot I wanter know, miss—wot mikes you think 'e thinks I done it?'

She hesitated, then answered, 'I ken my uncle. And if you hadna done it, why would he be afeard of you and the sergeant meetin'?'

'I see. But, if I 'ad done it—then 'e would be afeard, eh? . . . Why, miss, if I'd *done* it?'

She was silent, and he understood her silence. She knew by now, as well as he did, that her uncle had a job for him, and that he could not afford to let him wear handcuffs until the job was finished. But she did not know—and this was the queerest tangle of all—that Ben was as ignorant of the nature of the job as she was herself.

'Where's yer uncle now?' asked Ben, after a pause.

'I think the sergeant wanted him to see the body—I'm no sure,' she replied.

'Then 'e'll be back soon?'

'Ay.'

'That means we ain't got much time.'

'We?'

'Yus. See—I think I gotter tell yer somethink—jest ter clear yer mind a bit, like, though it won't be much.' She looked at him eagerly. 'And I ain't sure if yer'll ezackly like it.'

'But you'll risk that!'

'Yus. On'y—it means trustin' yer, miss?'

'You can! I'll sweer it—'

'Yer word's enough.' He took a deep breath, prayed he was doing right, and said, 'I'm up 'ere on a job. I dunno wot it is. But wotever it is, I'm stright, and I'm keeping stright, and—and Gawd 'elp me if yer uncle gits ter know I'm stright!'

There was a little silence. Then she asked, quietly:

'Do you mean, my uncle isna straight?'

'I mean, 'e mustn't know I'm stright.'

'Because, if you were straight, you couldna do the job he'll gie ye?'

'I've jest said I dunno wot the job is,' Ben hedged, futilely.

'But you ken it's nae straight job?'

'Well—see—I said, didn't I, yer wouldn't like it.'

He turned his eyes away from her grave face. He had tried to ease her burden a little, and felt he had only added to it. A touch on his shoulder brought his eyes back. She had got up from the chair and she was standing before him again.

125

'I ken weel my uncle isna straight,' she said, in a low voice, 'and if it's money he's wantin', there's naething he willna do—short of murder. You'll hae no cause to regret what you've told me, Mr Wilkins.'

'I reckon *you're* stright, orl right,' mumbled Ben, fighting sudden emotion.

'I was more fortunate wi' my parents than wi' my uncle,' she replied, with a faint smile. 'Will you tell me ane mair thing?'

'Wot?'

'How is it you're—doin' this?'

'Oh! Well, that's a bit of a yarn—but it started in Lunnon—on a bridge—when I was torkin' to a detective as close ter me as wot you are . . .' The memory rose in his brain, filling it. Queer, how it kept coming and going. The detective seemed actually to be in the room, young, eager, alive—real nice young chap . . . ''E got shot, so I thort I'd carry on.'

He stared at her. There were tears in her eyes. Silly fool, he was!

'Nah, doncher worry, miss,' he said, patting her shoulder. ''E'll be orl right in the end!'

'Who?'

'Eh? Yer uncle.'

A smudge passed swiftly along the window-curtain. The front door opened and closed. Then the parlour door opened, and MacTavish stood before them. He seemed to have brought the cold mist in with him.

'Ah, so you're doon,' he exclaimed, brusquely. 'Weel, that's a guid thing, Mr Wilkins, for there'll be nae mair waitin'—we're awa this minute!'

126

16

Ben Murders Himself

The news came as a bombshell. It was obvious that the Black Swan was no longer healthy for Ben, but he wanted more than a minute to think about it. MacTavish, however, was not in a mood for delay. Turning to his niece he told her peremptorily to be off, and as she began to move hesitatingly towards the door he swung back to Ben and exclaimed:

'Did you hear me?'

'I ain't deaf,' retorted Ben, 'but wotcher want me to do? Shoot aht o' the winder?'

'That wouldna be too quick!'

'Wouldn't it? Well, it would fer me, see? I wanter know a bit more abart the posishun!'

The innkeeper glared. Then his nervously impatient features twitched into a mirthless grin.

'Ay! The position!' he said. 'Weel, Mr Wilkins, this is the position. A mon's wanted by the police for the murder of Mr Wilkins! And I'm askin' nae questions!'

A gasp came from the doorway. Despite instructions, Jean had lingered. Her uncle sprang round.

'Did I no tell you to go to the kitchen?' he exclaimed fiercely.

He seized her arm roughly. Ben wondered, through a dangerously red mist, whether he would ever be wanted for the murder of Mr MacTavish.

'Leave 'er be!' he cried.

'What's this?' fumed MacTavish.

'Wot I sed! Leave 'er be—or yer won't be arskin' nobody no questions!'

Astonishment and infuriation swept across the inn-keeper's features, but he dropped her arm, and all at once Ben understood his obedience. Jean had implied that her uncle was not a killer, but that he believed Ben was one. That gave Ben a certain advantage!

'You think you're somebody!' muttered MacTavish.

'Yes, and *you'd* better, too!' retorted Ben. 'Wot mikes 'em think I've killed Mr Wilkins?'

'Dagont, will ye wait here and be caught?'

'That wouldn't be nice fer you, sime as me, so wot abart gittin' on and tellin' me wot I'm arskin'?'

'Before the lass?'

Ben thought for a moment. He certainly wanted Jean to hear her uncle's information, but would Charles Wilkins or Harry Lynch or whoever he was now supposed to be, want her to hear? The moment was not long enough to unravel the tangle, but it was long enough for Jean to lend a hand.

'I've haird enough frae ye baith!' she said.

She left the room quickly and closed the door.

While Ben stared after her, MacTavish drew a long breath, then wiped his forehead with a large coloured handkerchief.

'Now, listen,' he muttered, 'and after you hae listened, show the guid sense a mon in your position would be showin'. Ay, and here is some mair aboot the position! I went to see the body. 'Tis the Lord's mercy it wasna brought here! They had found something mair. In the turn-up o' his trousers. A wee bit card—juist like the ane you showed me. Now d'ye ken why they're sayin' the dead mon is Mr Wilkins?

'I'm askin' nae questions, I'm askin' nae questions,' he went on quickly. 'I'm keepin' to my business, and I ken naething aboot yours when they dinna run side by side, as you might say. But naebody's seen you come, and here is the mist sent us so that naebody will see you gang. There's juist Jean, and I'll see *she* doesna open her mouth. So now we'll be awa', unless you're in a mood to waste *mair* time?'

'Where are we goin' to?' asked Ben.

'You ken that yoursel' as fine as I do,' he retorted. 'We're goin' awa' *to finish the business*!'

The final lap! It seemed impossible! Ben had begun to regard his road as one without ending. But there was an atmosphere of finality in MacTavish's attitude which informed him that somewhere in the white maze around Muirgissie lay the conclusion of his adventure at last. And, very probably, of himself, also.

So he grunted, 'O.K.—carry on!' and placed himself in the innkeeper's hands.

The departure was effected with swift stealth. In less than three minutes Ben had been conducted to a yard, had entered a closed car that vied in age with the late Mr Smith's, and had begun the last stage of the mysteriously ordained journey. Another journey was to follow it, but that was outside the original programme.

He had been disturbed and disappointed that he had not seen Jean again. He would have welcomed a few more words with her, but if she had tried to secure another meeting the attempt had failed; as indeed it must have, since MacTavish did not let Ben out of his sight for more than two seconds at a time. Thus he merely had an incomplete and tantalising memory to accompany his thoughts and comfort his needs as the car progressed slowly but steadily through the shifting whiteness.

Neither driver nor passenger spoke for several minutes, and Ben had plenty of time to ponder over the new situation. The pondering brought him no balm, however, nor did it bring clarity. His mind was as misty and as uninformative as the view. Behind stretched an ever-lengthening road punctuated with ever-increasing obstacles. Ahead, the road remained a mystery. When he solved the mystery—if he ever did—how would he be able to retrace the road and negotiate the obstacles? Law and lawlessness would both be pitted against him, each endeavouring to give him the k.o. One or other would be bound to do it. And there would not be a single mourner to send him a wreath!

Well—perhaps Jean?

''Ere, shurrup!' he rounded on his thoughts. 'Do yer know wot yer gittin'? Merbid, that's wot you are—merbid! Lumme, didn't Shikespeare or some'un say orl the world was a blinkin' gime, and 'owever it goes, yer ends up unner the earth? So wot are yer worryin' abart?'

His attempt to set aside worry was not assisted by the more immediate details of the journey. The road was winding steadily upwards, and although MacTavish was not achieving any speed records, he was driving faster than appealed to Ben's breakfastless stomach. The higher you go, the farther you can fall, and several times the car's wheels seemed perilously near the edge. Further inconvenience was occasioned by a stack of boxes and cases piled inside the car, and filling practically all the room not occupied by the driver and his passenger. Once a case toppled, and landed on Ben's back.

'Wot's in 'em?' inquired Ben, breaking the silence at last. 'Bricks?'

'Stores,' replied MacTavish.

''Oo for?'

'Wha do you think?'

'Is this a derliverin' van?'

MacTavish smiled dryly.

'And why no'?' he answered. 'If I do a body's shoppin' for him, and deeliver every aince in a while, why am I no' doin' the same the noo?'

'I see,' replied Ben. 'On'y this time yer deliverin' me as well as the beer! Well, if yer tike the next corner as quick as yer took the larst, yer won't derliver nothink.'

'Dinna fret, I ken this road upside doon, though there's nae many can say the like.'

'Well, I'd rather ken it right-side up,' commented Ben. 'Then ter-day's derliverin' day, is it?'

'Nae alternative,' responded MacTavish, with a frown, 'but it's a pity I couldna mak' certain it was convenient.'

'Wot's that mean?'

'There was nae time to arrange matters, as I'd 'a prefaired.'

'Oh! Then ain't we expecked like?'

'Ah, weel, I'm no sayin' it will mak' any differ. Will ye talk a wee bit less, do you mind? There's a loch a thousand feet below us, though you canna see it.'

'Wot, a like?'

'The same you saw at Muirgissie.'

'Yer wrong—I carn't see in the dark no more'n I can in the fog.'

'It was juist across the road.'

'Well, you orter know. But, look 'ere—'ave we gorn up a thahsand feet?'

'And there's mair yet. You're missin' a grand view, Mr Wilkins, I'm thinkin'.'

'Well, see we go on missin' it,' said Ben. 'I don't wanter be turned inter a bit o' scenery!'

The road continued to ascend. It grew narrower and rougher, and the stretches without twists and turns grew shorter. Occasionally they dipped down disconcertingly, and each time Ben thought, 'That's done it,' to discover a moment later that it had not. There was one half-mile when the mist thinned, but the view was so desolate and rugged that Ben was grateful to re-enter the thick curtain again.

Presently, the car stopped.

'Are we there?' asked Ben.

'Nigh enough for a talk,' answered MacTavish, and took out his pipe.

Ben watched him carefully, sensing that something was coming. He was learning MacTavish, and could read the signs.

'Wunner if 'e's got me up 'ere fer a gime of 'is own?' he reflected. 'P'r'aps 'e's bin bluffin' me orl the time, and 'e ain't tikin' me nowhere!' The disconcerting thought was followed by another more consoling. 'Any'ow, 'e thinks I did Mr Smith in, so I better see 'e goes on thinkin' it fer a bit!'

Now MacTavish was puffing at his pipe. Suddenly he puffed himself to the point.

'Weel, Mr Wilkins, or whatever your name may be,' he said, 'whaur do you keep it?'

'Keep wot?' replied Ben.

'You ken fine wha' I mean,' answered MacTavish.

'Yus, and you'll ken fine wot I mean if yer don't speak pliner,' retorted Ben. 'As fer me real nime, if I was to tell yer that, yer'd fall in a swoon!'

'Maybe it's Crippen?'

'Worse'n that. So git on with it!'

MacTavish looked at Ben down his nose. It was a long nose, and a long look. Then he said, in a slightly more propitiating voice:

'I'm thinkin' you and me can talk guid business, Mr Wilkins?'

'Let's 'ear the business,' returned Ben.

'Ay,' nodded MacTavish.

'And when I ses that,' went on Ben, 'I mean cards on the table. Yer ain't dealin' with no ordin'ry bloke, don't fergit, and perhaps, fer orl yer might think, I knows more'n I pertend. I reckon hactin' comes nacheral ter both of us—eh?'

MacTavish considered the little speech. He was not unimpressed. After two or three more puffs, he appeared to come to a decision with himself.

'A' right—cards on the table,' he nodded. 'And here's the fairst card. When you came last evenin' I was cautious. It was necessary. "Wha is he?" I said. "Is he juist anybody, or is he Wilkins?" I waited for the proof.'

'And I give it yer,' said Ben.

'Ay. So then I said, "Ay, he's Wilkins. In the mornin' I'll

gang to—a sairtain person—and we'll arrange the meetin'. And he'll hand it over, and nae doot mak' his wee bittie, and I'll mak' my wee bittie.'

He grinned. Ben listened hard. The phrases, 'Whaur do you keep it?' and 'Hand it over,' revolved round his mind. Something, at last, was forming . . .

'Weel, then—'

''Arf a mo',' interrupted Ben. 'It's my turn to arsk you a thing or two, and then yer can go on.'

MacTavish looked slightly worried by the interruption. Ben was developing an idea that his companion, at root, was no braver than Ben himself.

'I slep' very sahnd larst night,' said Ben. 'I don't s'pose nobody dropped nothink inter me apple-pudding, did they?' Now the inn-keeper looked more than a little worried, and Ben added quickly, lest MacTavish should dry up, 'Well, I ain't blimed nobody yet, 'ave I? I can give a nice little sleepin'-draught meself when I think a bloke's tired—like I was, see?—ter mike 'im drop orf sudden arter a bit of a jaw. And ter let 'im sleep sahnd so's 'e won't be woke up by no noises if anybody should come inter 'is room.'

'I'm no understandin' you, Mr Wilkins,' muttered MacTavish, looking rather pasty.

'That's orl right,' replied Ben. 'Carry on. Yer was decidin' ter tike me over ter this certain person in the mornin'—like yer now doin'.'

MacTavish waited a few moments, to remarshal his wits, and then resumed:

'You're no' richt. I decided to see the sairtain person fairst mysel'.'

'Oh, yus.'

'But I had to change the plan.'

134

'Why?'

'Ah, you ken that!' exclaimed MacTavish, nervily. Then quickly grew calm again. 'I couldna leave you behind, after—after wha' was discovered, could I?'

'Yer mean, the deader?'

'Wha else would I mean?'

'Wot I'm s'posed ter 'ave done in?'

'I'm nae supposing anything! But—the sergeant would 'a supposed it—and you'll mind I didna gie him the chance. But if, noo—if the sergeant would 'a been richt, why then aince again I'd 'a been wrong in my thinkin' aboot ye—for, after all, you couldna be Mr Wilkins if you'd killed Mr Wilkins, now, could ye?'

'I see,' answered Ben. 'Orl right, nah let's do a bit more s'posin'. S'pose I killed 'im, wot am I s'posed to 'ave killed 'im for?'

'The sergeant wouldna ken that,' smiled MacTavish.

'But *you'd* know, eh?'

MacTavish's smile was now almost pitying.

'Ay, I'd know,' he agreed. 'Mr Wilkins has a wee matter o' ten thousand pounds on him.'

Ben kept very still. Ten thousand pounds. Ten thousand— Lumme! . . . Where was it?

The answer came in a startling flash of illumination. All at once Ben remembered something he had entirely forgotten in the stress of new considerations and events. In his last minute with Mr Smith, Mr Smith had said, 'Just one more thing . . . The post office . . . One can always call for letters at the post office.' And then he had dropped a card with Charles Wilkins's name on it. No, two cards, although he had only regained one, the other having slipped into the turn-up of his trousers! One card was meant for

135

Ben's identification with MacTavish; the other, should MacTavish retain his card, for identification at Muirgissie post office, where a packet containing ten thousand pounds was waiting at this moment for Mr Charles Wilkins . . . when he called . . . if he called . . .

'Yus, and 'ow *can* 'e call?' thought Ben. 'If I goes there nah I'll be 'ad up for bein' murdered! Gawd, that's fair done it!'

Doubtless there were instructions with the money. He would now have to turn up at his final destination without either. Chaos was complete!

17

Consultation in the Mist

'Weel?'

MacTavish's voice recalled Ben from conjecture to fact. Of course—MacTavish was sitting beside him, smoking a pipe. Asking him about a little matter of ten thousand pounds!

Forget the rest for the moment—think only of MacTavish—how to deal with MacTavish. Desperately Ben sought the next move in this complicated game, while the innkeeper watched him closely with a queer unpleasant leer. Suddenly the next move dawned, surprising in its simplicity.

'Corse, it's orl very interestin', Mr MacTavish,' said Ben, 'but yer ain't on'y up a mountain—yer up a pole.'

MacTavish raised his shaggy eyebrows and waited for further enlightenment.

'Yus, right on the top of it, like the monkey,' continued Ben. 'I let yer go on fer a bit becos' I wanted ter see where yer was gittin' at, but—wot, me murder 'im? Yer looney!'

MacTavish said nothing.

'Not that I mind a little thing like murder,' Ben went

on, deciding it might be wise to express a belief in the general principle, 'and not but wot p'r'aps I ain't done five or six put-aways in my time—but I'll tell yer why yer looney abart *this* 'un. If I murdered the bloke, I murdered 'im fer 'is money, didn't I? And if I'd murdered 'im fer 'is money, I'd 'ave gorn orf with 'is money, wouldn't I, instead of callin' at an inn jest ter pass the cash on? Likely I'd tike a trip over a lonely mountain with a nice honest feller like you!'

MacTavish began to look depressed.

'And 'ere's another thing wot yer looney abart,' added Ben, driving his points home for all they were worth. He had MacTavish in a descending mood. 'Do yer think that the brines wot's at the bottom o' this little bizziness would let Mr Wilkins spend a night at your 'ome from 'ome with ten thahsand pounds on 'im? See, they'd say 'e might lose it in the night!' Ben was interpreting the brains correctly. 'So they'd find a way—*not* ter be told yer—of keepin' that money secret. It ain't on me, Mr MacTavish, nor it wasn't on the bloke wot's been killed, so nah yer can tike yer choice!'

'Then—wha *was* the mon—they found?' asked MacTavish, breaking silence at last.

'I can tell yer that too,' answered Ben. ''E was a feller I 'ad no more cause ter kill than I 'ave ter kill you. I knoo 'im by the nime o' Smith, though I never knoo 'im at orl not till yesterday mornin'. 'E drove me from Boston ter Muirgissie—leastwise, orl but the larst mile. Then 'e dropped me, and seemed in a 'urry ter git back, but 'e pertended 'e 'ad some other bizziness in Muirgissie fust, so 'e went on a'ead to a turnin'—and it was there I fahnd 'im.'

'Dead?'

'Well, not livin'.'

'Why didna you tell me?' exclaimed MacTavish.

'Becos' I ain't a mug,' returned Ben. 'We 'ad ter git acquinted, didn't we?'

MacTavish frowned, but accepted the explanation.

'Wha aboot the card?' he asked.

'Ah, there yer've got me guessin',' admitted Ben, 'but 'ow abart this fer a shot? 'E give me one card—ter show you— but p'r'aps 'e orter've give me two and lorst the other in 'is turn-up? If that ain't it, I can't tell yer.'

'It's a possibeelity,' nodded MacTavish. 'But there's ane question still to be answered.'

'Yus. 'Oo *did* it?'

'Ay!'

'Well, I wasn't given a seat fer the performance, so this 'as gotter be another guess. S'pose you 'elp me this time? I sed this chap Smith drove me, didn't I?'

'You did.'

'And when I fahnd 'im dead 'e was in the car.'

'Weel?'

'Did the pleece find 'im in a car?'

'They didna.'

'Then where's the car?'

'Maybe they tipped 'im oot and drove awa' in it.'

'That's wot they did,' said Ben.

'Ye ken that?'

'Yus. And 'ere's somethink else I ken. They drove past yer inn, and they stopped at the inn, and looked through the parler winder, and then drove orf agine—jest afore you come back yerself. I wasn't quick enough ter see 'oo it was, but I spotted the car and reckernised it. And then you comes along, Mr MacTavish,' Ben went on, 'and you

arsks me, "Was it a woman?" So now I'm arskin' *you*—
'Oo's the woman?'

MacTavish stared. Ben almost pitied him, he was so
different from the hectoring man who a few moments ago
had tried to bluff him. His face seemed to have caught the
whiteness of the mist.

'Yes, and 'oo was in yer garden larst night,' Ben added,
''idin' in a bush?'

'The garden!' exclaimed MacTavish. 'Wha did you see
in the garden?'

'I dunno as I saw nothink in the garden,' answered Ben,
'but 'earin' sahnds I thort I saw a light, sime as it might be
a flash-torch, and then a bush movin', and arter that I 'eard
a door slam, and arter that—well, that was when I got
sleepy so sudden.'

He did not mention Jean's visit to his room—in case she
had not.

'Ay, I haird the sounds, too,' replied MacTavish.

'Was it you wot banged the door?'

'Nae, that was the wind! I was searchin' round the hoose
and the garden—'

''Oo for? The woman?'

MacTavish turned his head suddenly. The mist was now
thicker than ever; they were imprisoned in it. It blocked
the windows on either side, and had even swallowed up
the front of the bonnet.

'Wot's the matter?' asked Ben.

MacTavish did not seem to hear.

'Worse'n ever, ain't it? 'Ow are yer goin' ter git back?'

'Eh?'

'Yer know wot I think?' said Ben. 'I think yer'd better
tell me abart that woman.'

MacTavish removed his eyes from the window and fixed them on Ben.

'Mr Wilkins,' he said slowly, 'I'm thinkin' you're no an easy mon to read. I'm thinkin' you hae been gi'en this job because you're a remarkable mon. I'm thinkin' there's mair behind you than I gae ye credit for—'

'Lumme, 'ow much more's 'e goin' ter think?' wondered Ben.

'—and I'm no askin' to be told mair than you hae been instructed to tell me. But I reckon you can tell me this wi'oot givin' awa' ony secrets. It's aboot yoursel' I'm askin'. I ken fine the noo that you didna kill Mr Smith. But was it the truth when you drapped a hint that you'd killed—others?'

'Wotcher want ter know that for?' demanded Ben.

'I hae a guid reason.'

'Let's 'ave the reason.'

'I'll no gie the reason—but, maybe, it's for your protection, Mr Wilkins—maybe, ay!'

At that moment MacTavish looked almost human. Ben took a chance on it.

'I ain't never killed nobody in me life,' he replied, 'but that ain't sayin' but wot I couldn't!'

'Ah!' murmured MacTavish. 'Then noo I'll tell you aboot the woman.'

His pipe had gone out. He relit it. Then after another glance out of the window, he said:

'It was her came the fairst time. I brought her here blindfold. She didna like that. You'd 'a been blindfold yoursel' but for the mist, Mr Wilkins, only when you canna see anyhow, wha's the neceesity? There was a mon, too, but he stayed behind. I'm thinkin' it was juist as weel!'

141

'Wot was they like?' inquired Ben.

'Like I dinna want to see again,' answered MacTavish fervently. 'He was a big mon, though I had aye a notion he was soft, and the woman—she had mair good looks than was good for her, ay, and maybe for others. But when she was talkin' business, then she was as hard as nails, and we soon found the business she talked was no to our likin'. Do ye ken wha' it was, Mr Wilkins?'

'You're tellin' the story,' replied Ben.

'And you're canny, though you're no Scottish,' retorted MacTavish. 'Weel, there's no need to conceal wha' I hae no doot you'll learn, and her business was murder.'

'Oh—like that, was it?' murmured Ben.

'Ay, murder,' repeated MacTavish. 'I mind her words, for I was present, but, bein' canny hersel', she didna use the term. "If you're gi'en the money," she says, "wha' guarantee hae we this will be the end on't it?" "You hae my word," he answers. "A word is like an egg," she says, "'tis easily broken." "Wha' mair can I do?" he says. "There's ane thing you can do," she says. "Wha' is it?" he says, though there was nae need to put the question. Some things are said plainer in the e'en, Mr Wilkins, than wi' the lips. "Will I put it in words?" she says to that. He didna answer, and maybe she didna understand his silence, for she said next, "Or I can hae it done for you."'

MacTavish paused to swallow.

'You should 'a seen him at that! He made me jump as weel as her. "Gang awa'!" he cried. "Gang awa'! I'll hae nae sic thing!" Havers, I thocht he was daft! "Ye ken my terms," he cries. "Gang awa'!" She tries to pacify him, but she could 'a pacified the ocean easier. "Forget it," she says, "and tak' me to the boy for a sicht o' him.' But he wouldna do that, though she said she wasna payin' the money until she kenned the boy was there. "Then I'll hae nae money frae you at all," he cries, "and I'll hae nae murderin' folk here! Awa' wi' ye, and tell them never to send you back again. If they're no sendin' a pairson I can deal wi', they'll ken wha to expect!"

'And awa' I took her—blindfolded again, but wi' her hands tied this time as weel, and why I wasna killed mysel' when I was hame and she was untied I canna say. But awa' they went, and I had my instructions to see they didna return . . . And noo *you* hae been sent, Mr Wilkins, and I'm wishin' you better luck!'

Somehow Ben kept his whirling head. His reply proved it.

'I knew orl that,' he said, marvelling at himself.

'Wha's that?' exclaimed MacTavish.

'Corse I did! I wouldn't 'ave bin sent 'ere by—you know 'oo—if I didn't know the lot, would I? But I 'ad ter 'ear yer tell it, ter mike sure yer wasna lyin'.'

'And why should I be lyin'?' demanded MacTavish indignantly.

'Lumme, there's times yer sich a mug I wunner yer carn't be bought fer a tanner at Woolworth's! Yer don't want no murder—'

'Eh!'

'—but when yer thort I'd done one jest now, yer was ready ter bargain with me fer a share o' the swag! Gorn, that mikes me trust yer!'

The thrust went home. MacTavish dwindled like a pricked balloon.

'You're richt,' he muttered, with almost pathetic

admission. 'Maybe—maybe the poseetion got on top o' me. But dinna think I was approvin' o' murder—'

'No, yer was jest sayin' wot's done's done, so let's mike a bit. I dunno wot they calls that in Scotland, but in England they calls it hexory arter the act. Well, we'll let that go, becos' we got quite enough ter think abart—'

'Ay!' interrupted MacTavish. 'And you ken wha we hae to think aboot?'

He stared out of the window at the wreathing mist, which showed no sign of abating.

'I bet I ken,' answered Ben. 'Wot we gotter think abart is the person wot *did* kill Mr Smith, ain't we? And 'oo may be aht in that there mist waitin' ter kill somebody else? Or, ter put it in pline words, this 'ere woman?'

18

In the Wake of MacTavish

Ben always thanked MacTavish for his immobility during the next few seconds. The innkeeper did not seem able to remove his eyes from the window, and kept them glued on the glass as though he were waiting for some unpleasant vision to materialise there. Meanwhile, Ben struggled to adjust himself to his new information, and to become as composed inside him as he was appearing externally. This was not easy, for in addition to his personal fears, he found himself battling against fresh indignation which included even greater fears for another. In fact, although his new information was not complete, and merely gave him definite pieces in an indefinite jigsaw, it was at this point that he might have attempted to establish personal contact with the police had the road back to a police station been clear.

But the road was blocked not only by the mist, but by shadowy forms which, as MacTavish himself believed, were liable to solidify at any moment. Moreover, while Ben knew that he was in the immediate vicinity of his destination, he could not yet identify it. The knowledge he possessed was tantalisingly insufficient.

It was queer—worse, it was emotionally devastating—how his centre of interest continually changed, or intensified, all along the route, and how the motives for completing the ominous journey increased to prevent him from running away. If he had appeared braver in his present adventure than in previous ones, it was because he had, in each new encounter, had to assume the pose of a man less terrified by life and death than Ben himself, and periodically he had slipped into the unsavoury protection of a false skin. But he was continually slipping out again, and when his own frightened soul became bare once more, some fresh personality was thrown across his path at each wavering point.

He would have run away at the very beginning of this adventure—he had actually tried to do so, on the bridge—if he had not suddenly been rendered too heroic by the contemplation of a contemptible murder. The vision of that motionless detective had lived with him a long while. Then, while unseen fingers were tightening around him, a poor idiot of a bloke called Smith had become as motionless as the detective, reinforcing his determination to continue into the Unknown and see the business through. Then a girl had tugged at his heart. 'Why?' he asked himself, almost indignantly. 'She ain't nothink ter do with me? If I was one o' them 'andsome 'eroes there might be some sense in it—I'd git 'er away to somewhere nice and we'd, well, marry or somethink silly. But if I do git 'er away, and 'ow am I goin' ter, it'll jest be Thank yer and Ta-ta! Like it always is!'

And now, added to the list of those Ben was to avenge or rescue, was a boy.

Somehow the boy seemed worst of all. The mere thought

of the little fellow hidden away in this mountain loneliness, with menace creeping closer and closer through the mist, made Ben feel sick. 'Yus, but why?' he again demanded of himself. ''E might be a little 'orrer!' It made no difference. The incentive to avenge the dead, though it had provided the original impetus to this exploit, was less strong in him than the incentive to help the living. After all, it was the living who needed assistance . . .

''Ere, wotcher doin'?' he jerked suddenly.

The car was slowly moving again.

'We canna stay here for ever,' grunted MacTavish.

'Expeck yer right,' replied Ben, 'but I'd sooner git aht and walk.'

'We'll be walkin' in a minute,' answered MacTavish. 'Juist bide a wee.'

The car groped its way forward. MacTavish had taken advantage of a temporary thinning of the white blanket around them. They climbed a hill at a snail's pace, wound across a small plateau, twisted into another hill, and stopped again.

''Ide Park Corner?' inquired Ben.

'We're gettin' oot here,' replied MacTavish.

''Ooray! Fur to walk?'

'Far enow on sic' a day as this!'

'That's right,' agreed Ben. ''Arf a foot's 'arf a foot too much this weather! Wot abart the cases?'

'We'll not be worryin' aboot them.'

'Fer show, was they?'

'Do you ken how many questions you've arsked since we started?' exclaimed MacTavish, with heavy exasperation. 'Will *you* carry ane o' the cases?'

'Keep yer wool on,' answered Ben. 'I likes ter know things.'

He opened the door, and stepped out into space.

Fortunately the space had a solid bottom, but there was no knowing how long the bottom would last. Not till he left the car did he realise how warm it had been inside.

MacTavish followed him out. The two shadowy forms remained still for a moment, trying to pierce the curtain.

'Vizzerbility nil,' commented Ben.

'Weel nigh,' answered MacTavish. 'If someone's standin' five yards awa', we'll no ken.'

'And they won't ken us either,' replied Ben. 'Which way do we go?'

'You go where I go.'

'Not if yer goes over the edge, I don't!'

'I'll no be goin' over the edge, and no more will you if you follow me.'

"Ere's 'opin'!'

They proceeded in single file. Ben hooked his eye on to MacTavish's lanky form and never let go. More than once he barged into the form.

'Mind my back!' complained MacTavish.

'Mind my front!' retorted Ben. 'Yer keep on stoppin'.'

'I only stop when I hae to!'

'Well, I on'y 'it yer back when I 'ae to! Give us a toot or somethink!'

A minute later MacTavish stopped again.

'Wot is it this time?' inquired Ben, disentangling himself.

'Whisht!' whispered MacTavish.

Ben listened.

'Do you hear anything?' murmured MacTavish.

'Yus!' muttered Ben.

'Wha' do you hear?'

'Nine men with carving knives.'

MacTavish exploded.

'I'm sick o' your daftness!' he exclaimed.

'And I'm sick of yer stoppin' and then goin' on and then stoppin' like a bloomin' bus!' retorted Ben. 'If we're bein' follered, that ain't the way to shike 'em orf, is it?'

MacTavish swore softly, and moved again. The next time he stopped was at a gate. Ben stared at the gate incredulously.

'Lumme, yer don't mean ter tell me we're 'ere!' he exclaimed.

'Ay, we're here,' replied MacTavish, 'but dinna move for a minute.'

Ben advanced his hand and touched the gate, to make sure it was real. It was not the gate to Paradise, but its solidarity gave him a sense of comfort amid this world of shifting space.

'Yer jest carn't stop stoppin', can yer,' he grumbled. 'Wot's this one for? Prayers?'

MacTavish did not reply. Ben turned his head. MacTavish had evaporated.

Ben settled himself to wait for the minute. It was a very long minute. A bit too long.

''Ere—where've yer got to?' he called softly.

MacTavish did not inform him.

''Ow long's a minute in Scotland?' he asked the emptiness. 'In England it's sixty seconds.'

A form began to materialise in the mist.

'Oh, there yer are,' said Ben.

The form vanished. As he stared into the void, trying to recreate the lost vision, a sound on the other side of the gate caused him to twist his head quickly back again.

'Well, sir, well, sir!' exclaimed a sharp voice. 'And what are *you* doing here?'

19

The Old Man

The speaker was an old man. He had perfectly white hair, and plenty of it, and as he leaned over the gate and regarded Ben with palpable suspicion, his bright eyes made little lamps in the mist.

'Ah—yer wanter know 'oo I am?' murmured Ben, trying to jerk himself back into efficiency, and not certain for the moment who he was.

'It would interest me,' answered the old man. 'I do not receive many visitors.'

'No, but p'r'aps yer expectin' a visiter ter-day, eh?' suggested Ben.

'Today?' The old man's interest obviously tightened, and the snow-white head came a few inches farther over the gate, to get a clearer view of this particular visitor. 'No one calls here without an appointment. Have *you* an appointment?'

'I've come a long way ter see yer—'

'And you have brought—something—with you?'

Ben hesitated. Events were rushing him along too fast.

He would have given all he possessed, which was not much of a price, for a breather. How far could he confide in this old man? Up to what point could he count on assistance and beyond what point would he encounter fresh obstacles? The one clear thing was that Ben's mind refused to function at this gate—sandwiched between threatening shadow and suspicious substance!

'There's been a spot o' trouble, sir,' muttered Ben, lowering his voice. 'Could yer let me in?'

The old man pulled the gate open and Ben shoved himself through. He might be going out of the frying-pan into the fire, yet the sound of the gate clicking behind him was momentarily satisfactory.

'Yes, but—are you alone?' inquired the old man, peering over the gate again, his limited view no longer impeded by Ben's form.

'Looks like it, don't it?' replied Ben.

Suddenly the old man made up his mind. He motioned Ben to follow, and began to leave the gate. There was no sign of any house, but this did not mean a house was not far off, for it was still impossible to see more than four or five yards ahead. Ben's impression, however, was that they walked a considerable distance before the dissolving white wall was replaced by a solid one. In a porch they halted, and the old man paused with his hand on a door.

'We get dangerous animals in this part of Scotland,' he said, 'so I carry a gun. You've no objection?'

'Would it mike any difference if I 'ad?' asked Ben.

'None at all,' admitted the old man; and, opening the door, shoved him in.

The door closed with another satisfactory click, though perhaps the click was not quite so satisfactory this time.

By the dim light struggling through almost opaque window-glass, Ben saw that he was in a large substantial apartment. For its dimensions it could have contained considerably more furniture, but its bareness gave it an austere simplicity that fitted or created its character. The objects that caught Ben's attention first were four tall brass candlesticks on a long refectory table, from which rose majestically four unlit candles.

Ordering Ben not to move, his host walked to the refectory table, struck a match, lit a pink taper, and with the taper lit the four candles.

The new illumination increased the solemn grandeur of the room. 'Mind yer, I don't say I'd care ter live in it,' Ben thought, 'but there's something abart it that gits yer. Or don't it?' What was the something? A sense of solidarity in a shifting world—of ordered quietness—of past history that could not hurt you because it was over? Whatever it was, it was beyond Ben's dictionary to explain.

As the candle-flames glowed to full stature, they flickered on the contents of another smaller table. Lying on their backs, and definitely dead, were half a dozen toy soldiers, their spears extending uselessly beyond their recumbent heads. Facing the slaughter were four other soldiers— standing, and definitely alive. Three formed a neat row, the fourth was in advance, holding a flag. The splendour of the flag made up for the fact that the fourth soldier had no head. Four soldiers, and one of them blind, had beaten six. 'Not bad goin',' thought Ben.

'You are fond of soldiers?' inquired the old man curiously.

'Eh? Well, toy 'uns,' answered Ben. 'See, I 'ad a box once.'

'Indeed?'

'That's right.'

'And what about toy weapons?'

'Eh?'

'Or possibly, as you have now grown up, real ones?' The old man had produced a revolver while Ben had been staring at the toy battle. 'Do you mind if I search you?'

'Yer goin' ter any'ow, so why arsk?'

The old man smiled as he approached.

'You are wise to waste no time arguing,' he said.

'Corse I am,' replied Ben. 'See, I know better'n you that there's no time ter waste. Yus, and if *you* was wise, yer wouldn't be wastin' it at this minute.'

'What do you mean by that, my man?'

'Well, fust, if I wanted ter pot yer, I'd 'ave potted yer long afore this. Second, I ain't bulgin' anywhere, am I? Corse, I might 'ave one o' them biby guns wot yer shoots through yer button'ole. Third or fourth, whichever it is, I told yer there was a spot o' trouble, didn't I?'

The speech had some effect. The old man paused, though he still regarded Ben warily, and kept his revolver gripped tightly in his thin white hand.

'What is your name?'

'I got lots.'

'Select one.'

''Ow abart Wilkins?'

'I fear it brings me no nearer to you.'

'P'r'aps I don't want yer no nearer, not till yer put that cannon away!'

'You are a most unusual man, Mr Wilkins. It is difficult to know how to take you. What I intended to convey was that your name—the one selected—is unfamiliar to me.

And it should be familiar. I should have been warned of this visit.'

'Corse yer should of bin, and course yer would of bin but fer the trouble yer don't seem int'rested in!'

'Let me hear about this trouble, then,' said the old man, 'and you may be seated, if there is time for that. But I confess I am surprised if you possess something else that deserves protection.'

'Eh? Oh—I see wot yer mean,' murmured Ben. 'Well—there yer are!'

What the old man meant was ten thousand pounds! Lumme, *that'd* make a bit of a bulge, wouldn't it? Of course, it might be in thousand pound notes.

'Now, then—this trouble,' proceeded the old man. 'Let me hear. And also how it is that you have come here by yourself? That will need some explaining, Mr Wilkins, and let me warn you that if there is any attempt to repeat a certain incident of which you are doubtless familiar—'

'There won't be,' interrupted Ben, and glanced again towards the soldiers.

The old man watched him intently. Suspicion seemed decreasing, but he never loosened his grip on the revolver.

'And I *didn't* come 'ere alone,' said Ben.

'What!' exclaimed the old man. His voice sounded suddenly too loud. 'What?' he repeated, more softly, as though to correct the volume.

''Ow could I of, even if there 'adn't bin no mist?' He added, hoping this might further establish his bona fides, '*I* didn't 'ave ter be blindfolded!'

'MacTavish brought you?'

'Yus.'

'How?'

'Gawd knows! In 'is car.'

'I saw no car—'

'Corse not! Fust, you couldn't of, second, it wasn't there. See, we walked the larst bit.'

'I did not see MacTavish, either,' said the old man.

'Ah, now we're comin' ter it,' answered Ben. ''E come with me as fur as the gate, and then 'e ses, "Wait a minute," and vanishes.'

'Well?'

'Wot I sed. Vanishes.'

'Please be more explicit!'

''Oo?'

'Come, come, what happened exactly? A man does not suddenly vanish—'

'Well, I'm tellin' yer. I waited fer 'im ter come back, but 'e didna. Didn't. I wonders if 'e's gorn back ter the car fer somethink 'e's fergot. And then I thinks I sees 'im in the mist. And then you comes along. And then the person wot I thort was 'im vanishes. And 'ere we are!'

The old man frowned.

'I am not at all sure that we are "here," as you describe it!' he retorted. His suspicions appeared to be returning. 'MacTavish brings you here, and disappears outside my gate! Do you realise, my man, that—that some people might regard your story as thin?'

'Wot for?'

'You have no idea?'

Ben considered, then got the idea.

'Yus, I see. Yer mean I might 'ave used 'im ter git me 'ere, and then tipped 'im over the edge or somethink? That's right. And, 'avin' done that, I walks in this room like a blinkin' lamb, and lets you point a gun at me stummick. Why shouldn't *I* 'ave the gun and be pointin' it at *your* stummick, if I was the sorter bloke wot I'd 'ave ter be ter do wot I'm s'posed ter done? And then, if I'd pushed 'im over, 'oo was the other person wot vanishes? Did I push 'im over, too?'

'You really are a most—a most difficult person,' answered the old man testily. 'I did not understand that the second person was MacTavish?'

''E wasn't.'

'Then—'

''Oo was 'e? Ah, now we're comin' ter it!'

'We are continually coming to it!' rasped the old man. 'But we never come!'

'Well, now we *are* comin'!' promised Ben. 'I couldn't see 'im proper, it was orl too quick, but if 'e was 'oo I thort 'e was, 'e was a chap wot we thort was follerin' us.'

'Following you? What for?'

'Thort yer might guess.'

'You mean—? But surely you have not been such a fool as to let anybody know what you have brought here?'

''E carn't git orf that!' reflected Ben gloomily, as he replied, 'That's not wot I meant.'

'Then, for the good Lord's sake, speak plainly! I am getting tired of your riddles!'

'Riddles—lumme, that's right! But this orter be a easy one for yer. Wot's mikin' yer carry that there pistol?'

'Are you suggesting I have no need for my suspicions?'

'Wot I'm sergestin' is that yer so suspishus, yer carn't see no further'n me! Wot yer've gotter be suspishus of is this 'ere bloke I'm tellin' yer abart. Yer sed jest now there wasn't goin' ter be no charnce o' wot 'appened larst time. Well, s'pose this chap 'as bin follerin' me—yus, orl the way from

Lunnon—ter see if 'e can mike it 'appen this time? I'm arskin' yer? And s'pose 'e's got a woman with 'im?'

The old man quivered as though an arrow had passed through his body.

'And where's MacTavish?' concluded Ben.

He was thinking aloud as well as giving information. He found, to his surprise, that he could do so. He was covered by a revolver, but a few toy soldiers on a small table seemed to be holding it in check.

Suddenly the revolver ceased to cover him. The old man had slipped to the front door. He opened it a crack, poking his head out, and as he did so mist crept in. He closed the door, and went to the window. Then he returned to Ben.

'Who sent you?' he demanded.

That was a difficult one. While he hesitated the old man repeated his question sharply. Ben tried the truth.

'The woman,' he said.

'What!' exclaimed the old man.

'If I was actin' for 'er, would I tell yer?' retorted Ben.

The old man threw up his hands.

'Are you clever or a fool?' he asked.

'Bit o' both,' answered Ben. 'But I wouldn't be sich a fool as ter let on if I'd come 'ere ter do wot yer afraid of!'

'That might not be the admission of a fool, but of a man with a cunning brain?'

'That's right.'

'What do you mean, "That's right"?'

'Wot yer sed. Lumme, wotcher want me ter say? Fust I'm wrong if I ses wot I think, and then I'm wrong if I ses wot you think! If you'd bin through wot I've bin through in the larst week, yer'd be surprised yer 'ad any think left at all!'

157

'Come, come, don't—don't flare up like that! If you are not acting for the woman—and, I am bound to admit, it would be very good acting—who are you acting for?'

That was another difficult one. The truth this time might not be quite so easy to adjust. Yet suddenly Ben found a truth that seemed to fit the situation.

'Wot abart a little boy?' he suggested.

The reply very plainly astonished the old man. He stared at Ben with a totally new expression. Apprehension remained in it, but its texture changed.

'You are acting—for *him*?' he asked, dropping his voice.

'Yus,' nodded Ben.

'But you're not—you can't be thinking of—?'

He paused, torn with fresh doubts.

'Thinkin' o' wot?' inquired Ben.

'Taking him away?' The old man's agitation grew. 'You—you can't do that!' he exclaimed. 'That is—not unless— He is quite contented here, quite contented! If you take him back it will be madness! Only, of course—one must live, one must live—and in some comfort—with some style!' He waved his hand around, as though indicating the comfort and the style. Then he darted closer to Ben, and asked:

'Where are you *really* from?'

Before Ben could reply, a soft tap sounded on the front door.

20

Someone at the Door

The old man turned to the door but he did not move towards it. He waited for the tap to be repeated. A tense minute slipped by, and the tap was not repeated. A minute of that sort was all Ben could stand.

'P'r'aps it was the wind,' he muttered, breaking the uncanny silence.

'Do you think it was the wind?' whispered the old man.

'No,' Ben whispered back.

'Then why suggest it?' murmured the old man. 'You do not get wind and mist together.'

Now the old man crept cautiously towards the door. It seemed to Ben, watching anxiously, that the wise thing to do was to creep away from the door, and in spite of the snub he had just received he offered a warning.

'Look aht!' he advised. 'Some'un may spring at yer!'

'Sh!' hissed the old man.

He clearly had no intention of permitting anybody to spring at him. Instead of opening the front door when he reached it he bent down, gently lifted the flap over the letter-slit, and peeped through. His eye remained at the slit for several seconds. Then he lowered the flap, straightened himself, and came back again.

'See anyone?' asked Ben.

'No one,' answered the old man.

''Owjer know?' inquired Ben.

'What do you mean? I would know if I had seen anybody, would I not?'

'Not in this mist, yer mightn't?'

'Then why did you ask?'

'In case yer did.'

The old man glared.

'Do you ever speak sensibly?' he exclaimed. 'The invisibility does not extend to the porch! There is no one in the porch!'

'Oh,' said Ben. 'Then 'oo knocked?'

Deciding that further conversation with Ben was useless, the old man went to the window without replying. The mist gave him little more than his own reflection in the glow of four candles, the flames of which made four illogical glows in the wiped-out garden. Then he left the window and, taking a key from his pocket, crossed to the second door of the room at the back. Unlocking it, he left the room, locking the door again after him.

'Wunnerful 'ow I'm trusted,' reflected Ben.

Well, though he was imprisoned once more, a prisoner at least has solitude for thought, and the first thought of this prisoner was the anomalous one that, after all, he was not imprisoned. Only one door was locked. The other was his to open—if he chose to open it.

The question was, did he choose? Probably the old man had assumed that the answer would be an obvious negative—that the mist and its menacing secrets would form as secure a wall as a locked door.

'Corse I ain't goin' ter open it,' decided Ben, deriding the idea.

For how could he possibly profit by the audacious operation? If no one was there, as the old man had said, it would be waste of time, and if someone was there it would be madness!

'But there must 'ave bin some reason fer that there tap,' thought Ben. 'It'd settle yer mind like if yer knew it.'

He discovered he was walking towards the door. He stopped the moment he discovered it. One of Ben's troubles was that the various portions of him lacked co-ordination. This was why he had once nearly prostrated a dancing-instructress. His mind did one thing while his body did another, and often his body disagreed even with itself. More than once his legs had run away while his fists were heroically hitting.

Now his mind and body went through a tussle. It was a confusing tussle because neither could decide which side to take. He reached the door while the unsatisfactory argument was still raging.

Well, being there, he might as well follow the old man's example and take a peep. No, he wouldn't open the door. He would just take a peep. Not even a long peep. The old man had risked a bullet or a hooked nose, and Ben was not going to risk either. Just a quick squint—bing there, bing away again. You know—just *in case* MacTavish was outside, needing a hand . . .

'Mind yer,' thought Ben, "e's a durn rotter, if ever there was one, and the way 'e was ready ter share blood-money turns yer sick. I mean, when yer the uncle of a gal like 'is

161

niece. Corse, a uncle ain't so close . . . but if 'e's 'urt or anythink, and 'ad a tumble . . .'

Bing there! Bing away again! And, as the first bing proved satisfactory, as far as one could judge from its short duration, bing there again!

''Ooray!' thought Ben. 'Nothink but a draught!'

No, two draughts. One in his eye, and another at his feet. The other came through a crack under the door.

Ben removed his eye from the source of the first draught, and looked down at the source of the second. Vaguely, it disturbed him, because it gave him a new idea. Perhaps, if he lay down, he could get another squint of the porch, from a new angle. A squint along the floor of it. What good would that do? Well, if MacTavish, say—or anybody else, for that matter—had tapped, and then fallen, you mightn't see them from the letter-box, might you? But you might from the bottom crack, if they were on the ground.

Don't be silly! If there was a body on the ground on the other side of the crack, it would block the draught, and there wouldn't be any! . . . Don't be silly! It mightn't be plumb up against the crack, or it might only be blocking a part of the crack, and then there would be a draught, or part of a draught . . .

'Part of a draught,' repeated Ben in his mind. 'Wot's wrong with feelin'?'

He lowered his hand to the bottom of the door. Left half, draught. Good. Right half—where was the draught? Not so good.

''Ell,' he muttered, and went down flat.

As his hand had predicted, the left half of the crack was clear and white; the right half was blocked and dark.

Convinced now that MacTavish lay outside, and that

unless he opened the door at once he would never open it, Ben leapt up and turned the handle. An instant later the door was wide, and something slithered at Ben's feet. But the space ahead of him was a white blank, and the thing that had slithered at Ben's feet when the door against which it had leaned had been suddenly removed was not MacTavish. It was not, in fact, anybody. It was a packet.

'I'll be blowed!' muttered Ben. 'Postman?'

He bent down. If a postman had delivered the packet, he must have been a very knowledgeable postman. The name on the packet was the name of one Charles Wilkins, and there was no address.

Suddenly Ben raised his head from the packet. *Was* the space ahead of him a white blank? Or were there shadows in it? Seizing the packet, Ben closed the door quickly.

'Funny 'ow things git wuss when yer didn't think they could,' reflected Ben, as he stared stupidly at the packet in his hand. The packet had been stationary outside, but now it had a bad case of the wobbles.

Well, what next? Open the packet, he supposed. Bet something would go pop! Still, it had to be done.

Before doing it, however, he went to the window, stooping low as he went, and peered through the bottom edge for further evidence of those flitting shadows. All he saw was what the old man had seen before him—four stately candle-lights, reflected nonsensically in the misty garden. They were unpleasantly reminiscent of unwinking eyes.

He walked to the back of the room, deciding not to open the packet near the window. He chose the corner where the small table was. He didn't like fighting, even in fun, yet this toy battlefield was the warmest spot in the room.

He studied the writing on the packet, trying ostrichwise not to recognise it, but the instructions he had received from the chauffeur Fred before being passed on to Mr Smith of Boston rose with painful vividness in his mind. It was a bulky packet. Too bulky to have gone through a letter-box. Brown paper and string . . .

All at once he stopped staring at it and whipped the string off. He must open the parcel and digest the contents before the old man returned! In a trice the wrapping paper had been torn away and the contents were revealed. A box of chocolates, an envelope, and another small packet. The box of chocolates looked as incongruous in this room as the candle reflections out in the garden. Yet little boys who played with soldiers liked chocolates . . .

He opened the envelope, and read the note inside.

'The manner in which you are receiving this will prove that matters have not gone as smoothly as they should,' the note ran. 'But for bungling, you would have collected this at the post office, as arranged. Fortunately it was realised before the packet was posted that it could not be called for. You will have gathered already from certain incidents that bunglers are not given long to regret their errors.

'See that you give no cause now to regret any of yours.

'It is assumed that you have received and opened this discreetly.

'Tell your host, Mr Hymat, that you left the packet in the car, that MacTavish, who developed nerves, must have brought it to the door, knocked, and then returned to the car to wait for you.

'Actually, you will not be troubled any more with MacTavish.

'Give Mr Hymat the £10,000 in notes. He will expect it.

'Give the chocolates to the boy.

'Do not ask for any information that is not volunteered. Suggest that you are not interested. You are just doing your job, for which you are being paid, and the less you know the better. This, being the fact, can also be your attitude.

'But note that the giving of the chocolates is more important than the giving of the money. You are fond of children. You have some of your own, so know what they like. Make the boy promise to eat the chocolates himself— *and see that he does*!

'Do not be tempted yourself either by the money or the chocolates. Neither will do you any good.

'Do not attempt to leave the house until an hour after the boy has eaten his chocolates. Then report yourself at the gate with your news.

'If you fail, your work will be completed by others, and by other means, and it will be your last job. If you succeed, you will receive £50, as arranged, at the gate, and will be free to return to your own headquarters. We shall have no further use for you.

'But, till then, you can regard yourself as under observation.'

That was all. And quite enough.

Ben turned his head and glanced towards the door. How many were out there, keeping the other side of the door under observation? Three, he reckoned, at least. Miss Warren, Fred, and the mysterious Unknown, the Jack of Clubs. He did not include Mr Sutcliffe in the list. He could not picture that strange young gentleman outside the silent flat, or in any costume other than a dressing-gown.

He included the Jack of Clubs because he had long divined that his were the real brains of the party, and that those brains would not be far off at the crisis.

'Joe Lynch,' he thought, grimly, 'yer well out of it! Why, if I was really Joe Lynch, wot charnce'd I 'ave? If the old bloke didn't git me, or if the pleece didn't git me, those blighters out there'd git me—yus, if I succeeded or if I didn't! See *them* partin' with fifty quid when the job was finished! I'd be given a bullet, more likely!'

He turned back to the table with the soldiers. He looked at the prone warriors. Funny how people ran away from horror, yet how they enjoyed playing at it! But, of course, a little boy—he wouldn't have had a chance of learning yet, anyhow, would he?

'No, and 'e ain't goin' ter learn now,' muttered Ben, 'not if I knows it!'

'Don't move! Stand still!' piped a voice behind him. 'You're under fire!'

21

Development of a Game

With a curious sensation that the toy soldiers had suddenly come alive while the living enemy outside had died, Ben stood rigid. The speaker—by his voice some little distance in the rear—clearly had to be obeyed. After a few moments, during which the next move had to be decided on, the voice continued:

'You are my prisoner!'

'That's right,' answered Ben.

'What?'

'I sed, that's right,' repeated Ben. 'I'm yer prisoner.'

There was another silence. For some reason Ben's move did not appear the right one.

'Don't you mind?' demanded his captor.

'Not a bit,' replied Ben.

'Why not?'

'Cos' I knows yer treats prisoners proper and don't 'urt 'em.'

'But I might shoot you!'

'I knows yer won't.'

'How do you know?'

'I can tell by yer voice yer ain't that kind. Orl yer'll do is ter clap me in prison with a 'ot-water-bottle and give me jam fer tea.'

A very unmilitary sound issued from his captor, but the next moment it was swallowed by discipline.

'Let me see your face!' ordered the boy.

'It's a funny 'un,' warned Ben.

'Turn round!'

'I carn't.'

'Why not?'

''Cos yer told me not ter move.'

'Yes, but now I'm telling you to turn round!'

'Well, see, I'm a soljer, ain't I?'

'Are you?'

'Ain't I?'

'Yes.'

'Orl right, then is that the way ter speak to a soljer? 'Corse it ain't! Wot do yer say to a soljer when yer want 'im ter stop?'

'Halt!'

'Yus, well—'

'Right wheel!' cried the boy. 'Right wheel! 'Shun!'

Ben turned with such violent smartness that he nearly toppled over. His conqueror again emitted the unmilitary sound.

'There y'are!' grinned Ben. 'I told yer it was a funny 'un!'

Before him now stood a small boy with large dark eyes. Normally the eyes were serious, and even behind their present smile lurked a strange gravity. His hair, like his eyes, was dark, and his little body was very erect, although the gun that should have been terrifying the prisoner was held rather loosely.

He was standing in the doorway that led to the other portions of the house—he must have unlocked the door very quietly—and his outline, illuminated by the candles, was framed in the dimness of the hall beyond. But suddenly a second outline darted into the frame. The old man appeared behind him, his face white.

'Konrad!' cried the old man. 'Where have you been?'

The boy lowered his gun with a frown, but Ben answered for him.

''E's caught a prisoner,' he said. 'You're out o' this fer a minute, Mr 'Imat.' The old man moved his head sharply at the name. 'Tike my advice, and let 'im 'andle me—'e's doin' fine!'

'Why did you wink?' demanded the boy, his activity reviving abruptly.

''Oo wunk?' inquired Ben innocently.

'You did!'

'Go on!'

'I saw you!'

'Then I must of. It's a 'abit. Arter the Battle o' Waterloo. A cannonball 'it the top o' me eyelid and weakened the joint.'

The boy looked astonished. So did Mr Hymat. It occurred to Ben that perhaps he was becoming too flippant. He had a real game to play.

'Well, question the prisoner,' he went on. 'I might be a spy.'

'Are you?' asked the boy.

'Yus.'

'A spy!'

'That's right.'

'But spies are shot!'

There was a complimentary concern in the statement. Ben eased the situation.

'On'y when they won't speak,' he pointed out. 'See, I might 'ave some infermashun!'

He risked another wink over the boy's shoulder. The boy attributed it to Waterloo, but Mr Hymat, by his tense expression, realised that it had a more contemporary inspiration.

'Have you?' asked the boy.

'Yus, I 'ave,' replied Ben, 'so if yer shoot me yer won't find out!'

'What is it?'

'Must I tell yer, sir?'

'Yes, you *must*!'

'Orl right. It's abart the Enemy.'

'Ah! Where are they?'

'Ahtside!'

'What! In the garden?'

'Yus! And s'pose they looked in?'

The boy turned suddenly to Mr Hymat. Perhaps he wondered whether the old man was still interested in the game. It was obvious that the old man's interest was considerable.

'The Enemy must not see us!' cried the boy. 'Close the curtains!'

Mr Hymat obeyed with alacrity. While he was doing so, Ben observed:

'I can see yer know 'ow ter plan a battle. This ain't the fust one yer goin' ter win ter-day!' He glanced at the toy soldiers. 'Four agin' six, and beat 'em! So three agin' three orter be easy.'

'Do you mean there are three of the Enemy outside?' asked the boy.

'Well—that's wot I think,' answered Ben, glancing towards Mr Hymat.

'But *we're* only two,' said the boy.

'No, three,' corrected Ben. 'See, yer've got me, nah.'

The boy frowned.

'I don't like deserters,' he muttered.

'Well, strickly speakin', no more don't I,' agreed Ben, 'though sometimes yer can fergive 'em, yer know, the way they're treated.'

The boy considered the question of forgiveness, then shook his head gravely.

'*I* wouldn't desert, whatever anybody did,' he responded. 'They could boil me.'

'I'm with yer agine,' nodded Ben, 'on'y, see, yer've got *me* wrong. I ain't no deserter! I'm your side! I wouldn't desert, not if they stood me on me 'ead barefoot, and tickled me!'

'You say funny things,' smiled the boy. 'I think I'm glad you're not a deserter. But if you're not a deserter, why are you ready to fight on my side?'

'Ah!' murmured Ben, and glanced towards the old man. 'Yus, we *are* ready ter fight on 'is side, ain't we?'

'Eh—of course!' jerked the old man. 'What—what does that mean?'

'I'll tell yer wot it means,' replied Ben, while the effects of Waterloo once more registered themselves on his loose eyelid. 'It means that I've bin shoved inter this 'ere gime—wot we're orl playin', see?—and that when I'm shoved inter a gime I don't drop it not afore I seen it through. Yer wouldn't think it, not ter look at me—'

'I would,' interrupted the boy.

'Go on! Would yer?' exclaimed Ben. 'Orl right, that settles it! 'Cos when anybody *thinks* yer play the gime, well, then yer've gotter, ain't it? Yer on yer honour. So the gime this time is that—that the King's in dinger, see—dinger orl rahnd the plice, see?—and we've gotter git 'im aht of it. That's right, Mr 'Imat, ain't it? Nothink helse cahnts, not afore we've got 'im aht of it? Do yer tike me?'

A strange thing seemed to have happened to Mr Hymat. He stared at Ben harder than ever. But the boy laughed, and drew himself up.

'That's right, I'm a King!' he cried, 'and the Enemy's outside! But we'll beat them!'

'Corse we will—even if we 'ave ter retreat fust ter do it.'

'Kings don't retreat!'

'Sometimes they do. Kings retreat, it's the others wot run away.'

'But why should we retreat?'

'Well, you've gotter go on with yer questions ter find out that. I'm yer prisoner, but I ain't a deserter, so 'oo the funny bizziness *am* I?'

'Yes! Who are you!'

'One o' yer spies, yer Majesty!'

'Ah! A Royal spy!'

'Yus, yer Majesty.'

The boy saluted. Ben saluted back.

'What have you found out?'

'Well, see, I worked it like this. Now, listen careful, yer Majesty, 'cos it's a bit comperlicated. I ses, "I'll go among the Enemy," I ses, "and pertend I'm a deserter from the King's Army." See, by doin' that, I mide 'em think I was on *their* side, and so 'eard their plans.'

172

'Was that fair?' asked the boy doubtfully.

'Well, now yer arsk me, I ain't sure,' replied Ben, 'and if yer decide it wasn't, then yer must put me in prison arter I got yer sife, not afore, on'y don't fergit the 'ot-water-bottle, please, 'cos I git cold so easy. Any'ow, if it was fair or not, I'm jest tellin' yer. I found out—are we orl listenin'?—'

He turned for a moment towards Mr Hymat. Mr Hymat was listening as hard as anybody.

'I found out as they wanted ter send some'un in with—wotcher think—*poisoned sweets*!'

'What's that?' gasped Mr Hymat.

'There they are,' answered Ben, solemnly pointing to the box. It was on the small table with the soldiers. The packet of notes was beside it. 'So don't touch 'em, yer Majesty. As a matter of fack, I filled 'em with mustard,' he added confidentially, 'ter mike 'em more real like, so don't touch 'em any'ow. We'll chuck 'em away.' The boy looked disappointed. 'And git some new 'uns, eh?'

'What is in—the other?' asked the old man, lowering his voice and pointing to the packet.

'Ah, I'm jest comin' ter that,' replied Ben. 'The Enemy ses ter me, "Look 'ere, *you* do it," they ses, "'cos the King 'd never suspeck you." "Wot abart the old General?" I ses, "'e might suspeck?" "Well, if 'e does, bribe 'im," they ses, "and 'ere's ten thousand pounds in notes ter do it with. When you've give them to 'im, they'll keep 'im quiet!"'

'What, make *him* a deserter?' said the boy scornfully. 'They were very stupid!'

'Corse they was,' nodded Ben. 'But 'e wouldn't be so stoopid. Why, even if 'e could be bribed, wot's the bettin' the notes wouldn't be good 'uns, any more'n the sweets are?'

He squinted at Mr Hymat. The old man's forehead was damp.

'Not—good ones?' he muttered.

'Well—wot do you think?' inquired Ben.

Mr Hymat passed through a difficult moment. He became very red. Then he suddenly burst out:

'And what do *you* think? You know why I wanted the money—and that I wouldn't—'

He stopped abruptly, gasping. His voice had cracked. He darted a swift glance towards the boy.

'Corse I know,' answered Ben quietly. 'We're King's men, ain't we?'

Then he glanced towards the boy. But the boy was not attending to them. His eyes were on the window-curtain.

22

The Plan

'Do yer see anythink, yer Majesty?' asked Ben.

The boy put his finger to his lips and took a step towards the window, but Mr Hymat intervened.

'Stay where you are, Konrad!' he muttered. 'Don't come this side of the room!'

Konrad looked surprised at the reality of the command, then turned his head as Ben tapped him on the shoulder. Ben smiled into the large, wondering eyes while the old man, temporarily relieved of their embarrassing scrutiny, quickly mopped his forehead.

'We're playin' this gime proper,' explained Ben. 'See, like it was a play.'

'Yes,' answered Konrad slowly. His eyes were assuming a new solemnity. 'We're not the only ones who are playing it, are we?'

'Well, wouldn't that mike it more fun?'

'And there really are people in the garden, aren't there?'

'Didn't I say so?'

'I heard them just now.'

'Corse yer did! That's them walkin' up and dahn, like we told 'em to. See, we sed if we played the gime proper, they was ter do the sime.'

The boy nodded, and kept his solemn eyes on Ben's.

'Did the game begin before I came down?' he asked.

'Shouldn't wunner,' answered Ben. 'But 'ow did yer know that?'

'I was looking out of the window and I thought I saw a man in the mist, but I wasn't sure so I went in another room where I thought I could see better—'

'So that's where you were!' interposed Mr Hymat. 'I searched the house for you!'

'And did yer see 'im better from the other winder?' inquired Ben.

'No. He'd gone.'

'Wot was 'e like?'

'Very tall.' The boy raised his hand as high as he could. 'Taller than that.'

'Go on! And wot was 'e doin'?'

'Just standing.'

'That's right. 'E was s'posed ter be watchin'. I'm glad you saw 'im—the tall 'un—'cos I thort 'e wasn't goin' ter play. And arter you'd seen 'im from the fust winder, and then not seen 'im from the second, I expeck yer came dahn and caught *me,* eh?'

'Yes,' replied Konrad. 'At first, you know, I thought you were him, but that was silly, because you couldn't be.'

'No, *I* ain't a big 'un! Corse, yer reckernised it was a gime when yer saw me, didn't yer? When yer said, "Yer me prisoner"?'

'No.'

'Wot, yer really thort I was some 'un wot didn't orter be 'ere?'

'Yes.'

'Well, I'm blowed! Then yer was plucky speakin' ter me like yer did. Arter orl, that's on'y a toy gun yer've got there, and though I ain't very big, I'm bigger'n you!'

Konrad smiled.

'I'm a King,' he said.

'Lumme, I was fergettin'!' apologised Ben. 'So yer are. And kings 'ave gotter 'ave pluck, ain't they?'

'Yes.'

'But when yer saw me funny fice yer knew it was a gime, didn't yer?'

'It was when you said that about the hot-water-bottle. I mean, I knew then—I mean, yes, it was a game.'

He flushed slightly. It was the first time he had floundered. Even in these first moments of their acquaintance, Ben noticed that, when he was in doubt, he always thought first and spoke after his thinking.

'That's why I sed it,' winked Ben. 'So yer'd know. When a gime gits too excitin', I likes ter give meself a pinch now and agine ter mike sure it ain't real. Yus, and torkin' o' that,' he went on, 'don't fergit that wotever 'appens in this gime, it's bin orl worked out so that we win in the end, see?'

'I see,' replied the boy. 'Kings aren't frightened.'

He was standing very straight, but Ben wondered.

Ben himself was struggling with a fear that almost stifled him. This game had to be won, there was no argument about that, but the odds were heavily in favour of the Enemy; for outside were three keen and ruthless brains—possibly more—while inside were merely Ben's brain, a small boy's courage,

177

and an old man's impotence. True, in addition to a toy gun, they had a real revolver, but the weapons of the invaders were bound to be superior. Likewise, their ability to use them.

'Well,' said Ben, after a pause, 'now we'll git on with it and study the posishun.'

This produced another pause. No one seemed very clear about the position. It was the old man who offered the next contribution.

'Do you think they will try to get in?' he asked tremulously.

Mr Hymat was playing the game with a definite sense of realism.

'That's wot we gotter think abart,' replied Ben. 'But there's one thing we knows—they won't try ter git in not till they find out I ain't carried out their instructions and given 'is Majesty the chocklits wot we're pertendin' are poisoned.'

'When you are playing a game,' said Konrad, 'you mustn't use the word "pretend." You must do it.'

'That's right,' answered Ben. 'I fergot.'

'How long will it be before they know you haven't given me the chocolates?'

'Well, I should say, abart a hour,' replied Ben.

'Then we've got an hour.'

'Yus.'

'That will give us time to fortify the house. I know a lot of ways. I've got a tool-box.'

''E's a King, arl right!' exclaimed Ben approvingly. ''E's got ideas! But we must 'ear if the General's got any ideas, too.' He glanced towards Mr Hymat, who looked less a general than the boy looked a king. 'And then *I* might 'ave ideas. Wot we gotter do is ter orl say 'em, and decide which is the best. That's wot yer calls a Milerty Conf'ence.'

178

'But who are *you*?' inquired the boy suddenly. 'You haven't told us?'

'Yes, I did! I'm the Royal spy, ain't I?'

'Oh, yes.'

'King, General, Royal spy. I s'pose that *is* the lot?'

'There is no one else in the house,' said Mr Hymat.

'No servants, eh? Nobody wot could git a messidge through the Enemy lines?'

'There are only ourselves.'

'Well, that's less ter think abart, any'ow,' said Ben, 'and the smaller the numbers, the bigger the vict'ry!' He pointed to the six dead toy soldiers. 'But, torkin' o' messidges, wot abart a telerphone? Do yer git 'em in the mountains?'

'There is no telephone here,' replied Mr Hymat.

'Good! We're findin' out. Nobody ter send a messidge, and no telerphone. So we carn't—commernicate with the main army like. O.K.'

'Then it will have to be my idea,' said Konrad.

'I ain't so sure,' answered Ben. 'We ain't 'eard the General yet?'

Mr Hymat tried to drive his wavering wits into military channels.

'Yes, yes—barricade, by all means,' he muttered. 'Yes, certainly. But, if it really comes to that—if we are right in believing that the Enemy will actually attack—well, I suppose we are sure of that?'

'Wot you mean,' replied Ben, 'is that we orter look further a'ead? Am I right? Well, I'm with yer, General—if 'is Majesty don't mind me sayin' so. See, as we carn't git a messidge through ter the main army, p'r'aps we orter see if we could 'oodwink the enemy, and git through ter the main army ourselves? Git what I mean?'

'Not quite,' admitted Mr Hymat.

'We'll work it out, then, and see if *my* idea's any good. Mind yer, it mightn't be, but we're thinkin' of hevery-think, ain't we—and I've got an idea that would mike this the best gime that was ever played. There I go agine—I carn't fergit it's a gime, can I?'

He looked at Konrad apologetically, but this time he received no reprimand.

'Now, this is my idea,' he went on, 'but we gotter think abart it very careful, bit by bit like, sime as they did at Waterloo. "Doncher do nothink in a 'urry," Nelson ses ter me, "and then yer won't mike no mistake."'

'Wellington,' corrected the boy.

'So it was!' answered Ben. 'Nelson was Trefalger, wasn't 'e? I git 'em mixed up, bein' in both. Well, 'ere we are. Fust, I s'pose there's a back way out of this 'ouse?'

'There is,' replied Mr Hymat. 'But if we try that—'

''Old 'ard, 'old 'ard! I ain't finished yet! We couldn't git out o' the back door now, becos' it's watched, sime as the front door, but if we play a trick on 'em, then we could slip away, and the mist 'd 'elp us.'

'What trick?'

''Arf a mo'. I'm thinkin'.' He closed his eyes and thought. Suddenly he opened them. 'Lumme—I b'lieve I've got it. Yer carn't leave now becos' they're outside, but yer could if they was inside! So wot abart gettin' 'em inside?'

'Are you quite mad?' inquired Mr Hymat.

'I'll arsk you to tell me that when I've finished,' retorted Ben. 'Nah, listen! This is 'ow it goes. I'm s'posed to poison the King, ain't I?'

'So we understand.'

'That's right. And arter I've done it, I've gotter let the

Enemy know. "We've got to 'ave proof," they ses, "and don't you fergit it." Well, 'ow are they goin' ter 'ave proof if they don't come inside? So in they come. 'Oo let's 'em in? I do! And I shows 'em the box o' chocklets with 'arf a dozen gorn. Like this, see?'

He went to the box, took six out gingerly, and tied them up in his handkerchief.

'Corse, I gotter be careful now not ter blow me nose,' he smiled. 'Orl right. That's done. "Look there!" I ses. "That ain't no proof," they ses. "No, the proof's upstairs," I ses. "Where upstairs?" they ses. "In the Royal bedroom," I ses. And I tell 'em that there's where the King was, well, took ill, and that the General's took ill, too, becos' 'e 'ad a couple. Then up they goes, but they don't find nobody, becos' the King and the General 'ave slipped out at the back and are leggin' it fer orl they're worth. I mean, retreatin'.'

There was a silence, during which the plan was considered. Then Mr Hymat asked:

'Where do we retreat to?'

'Muirgissie, o' course! Once yer there yer can tell the pleece—that is, the main army.'

'They would follow us.'

'Well, yes, you'd 'ave ter race 'em, if I didn't find some way ted keep 'em back, but p'r'aps I would.'

The old man nodded. But the boy was frowning.

'What about you?' he asked.

"Oo? Me?' answered Ben. 'Oh, me.'

Yes, *what* about him? He closed his eyes again. All he saw this time was a rather unpleasant blank.

'Well, I ain't goin' ter tell yer abart me,' he said at the end of the profitless period. 'See, yer Majesty—that's goin' to be the surprise!'

23

Meanwhile, Outside—

'We manage these little matters better in my country,' said the tall man. He had a small pointed beard, but Konrad had not noticed that.

'There was a little matter you failed to manage ten years ago,' answered the woman beside him. 'A little matter on the other side of that door you're looking at! If you had, we shouldn't be standing here now, getting pneumonia in a Scotch mist!'

'That is true,' admitted the tall man. 'Except, I hope, the pneumonia. That was Rudolf's first failure.'

'And his last, Paul?'

He did not answer, merely giving a little shrug.

'We've plenty of fools in England—fortunately for the rest—but we haven't got a Rudolf! I hope the dear man is enjoying his reign!'

'Until recently—yes.'

'And since recently—no?'

'It has not been—your word is?—passive.'

'God, I should think not, from the sound of it!' murmured

the woman. 'Be careful, we mustn't talk too loudly. I suppose your Rudolf couldn't be satisfied with the normal fruits of office and tried killing the golden goose. And now the golden goose has turned.'

'And we are hoping to turn the goose back again,' murmured Paul softly, 'which we shall not do if it can find a new master.'

'You mean its rightful master!'

Paul removed his eyes from the door for an instant, and regarded his companion with surprise.

'You are not serving the rightful master, Helen—if our term is discreet?'

'I know that, I know that,' she muttered, under her breath. 'My goal's the earth, not heaven! But I object to fools, on principle!'

'Then why serve this one?'

'You ask that?'

They regarded each other. As he turned his eyes back to the door, he answered:

'It was a foolish question.'

'No, it wasn't,' she replied, rather wearily. 'Actually, I don't care a damn whether Rudolf's throne totters or not, but I've never been squeamish, and I took this on with my eyes open.' She gave a little harsh, ironic laugh. 'Wonderful what a month on the Riviera can do to a pure woman, isn't it?'

'Had I remarked the purity, the month would have been less wonderful,' he responded with equal irony.

'You do say the sweetest things! You must teach them to my tame lamb.' A fierce light shot suddenly into his eyes. She quelled it quickly. 'Don't be a child, Paul! You've had my promise—which I'll stick to if you stick to yours!

The simple truth is, my dear man, I've developed nerves up here for the first time in my life. I believe I shall have to retire to a convent.' She touched his sleeve. 'Isn't mist foolish to be wet?'

His eyes softened at her touch. She had intended them to.

'It has not been easy,' he conceded.

'Hardly child's play,' she answered. 'When accidents happen, I usually make a point of merely hearing about them.'

He nodded.

'It wasn't my own idea to come out on *this* trip!' she added.

'Or mine, to trust to strangers,' he said. 'You do not always pick so wisely.'

'Meaning?'

'Monsieur Fred, to begin—'

'*Prenez garde!* Monsieur Fred is not far off!'

'He is at the back.'

'He *should* be at the back. But he's not always where he should be! If he were five yards off at this moment we wouldn't see him, and he's a jealous brute—and hot-headed.'

'It is his hot head that will hang him,' remarked Paul contemptuously. 'He should be hanged three times already, I think.'

'The last occasion—just now—was with *your* approval!'

'So?'

'Don't prevaricate! And the second occasion was due to a fool you picked yourself.'

'It is true, our Mr Smith was too easily frightened—'

'Yes, if he hadn't pulled out his revolver, Fred would never have shot him.'

'If Fred had not frightened him by appearing so abruptly and unnecessarily, Mr Smith would not have pulled out his revolver. I am sure he produced the weapon for protection, not aggression. But Fred, as always, could not wait. And so, I understand from you, it was the first time when he shot the detective.'

'Quite right, Paul. I called him plenty of names for that. But at least he saved Joe Lynch for us.'

'Ah—Joe Lynch,' murmured Paul, contemplatively. 'Yes— Joe Lynch. I come to him in a minute. But there is another fool you have picked.'

'You can't forget Mr Sutcliffe, can you?'

'I may, when you do.'

'Forgive me for calling you an idiot, Paul, but at times you are. Probably this mist is clouding your sense, too! When we have completed our present business I shall forget Mr Sutcliffe, and Fred, and the whole bagful. Do you suppose I shall want them trailing after us across the Continent? I am turning over a new leaf in my book of purity, Paul, and you fill the page. Satisfied?'

'Thank you.'

She frowned a little as she regarded his almost irritating composure.

'You're a queer man, Paul,' she murmured. 'I wonder if that is why you attract me? No one would think there was any heat in *your* blood! Unless they knew you. Sometimes you're like a cold fish . . . Well, Joe Lynch. What about *him*?'

'That is what I am wondering,' he answered. 'He is a long time.'

'We're not wasting it. It's nice weather for a chat.'

'The one thing I do not understand about you is your

sense of humour,' he said. 'But that, after all, is just a strange English characteristic. The question is not whether we are wasting time, but whether he is. It is half an hour since he received his last instructions. The business could have been concluded in ten minutes.'

'I agree it could have been, not that it necessarily should have been.'

'You are happy, then, about Mr Lynch?'

'He is the oddest creature I have ever come across, but he seems to have carried out all our instructions so far.'

'I asked if you were happy about him?'

'If you mean am I certain about him, then no,' she retorted. 'I am not certain of anybody. Not even of you. If it suited your purpose, I have no doubt . . . well, never mind. But I told you of the tests I put him through. He could have given us away to a policeman—at least, he thought he could.'

'Did it occur to you, Helen,' asked Paul, 'that he might have realised it was a test?'

'Of course it occurred to me! But I was watching him very closely, and I know he believed Fred was a genuine policeman till the last moment. And don't forget, my dear, you were quite impressed yourself with his sleeping face!'

'It is easier to judge the faces of one's own countrymen. I wish, now, I had seen him with his eyes open. I accepted your judgment.'

'And now you don't?'

Before he could respond a figure loomed into view with startling suddenness. It grew like a rapidly developing smudge on a large white plate.

'How much longer have we got to wait?' demanded the figure.

It was the chauffeur Fred, who had arrived too late to hear doubtful compliments.

'We are wondering the same thing,' answered Paul, 'but you see we have not deserted our post.'

'Who's deserting any post?' frowned Fred.

'You are supposed to be watching the back entrance.'

'Yes, and I've watched till I'm sick of it! Even if anyone did slip out of the back door the moment I left it for a second—and why should they?—they'd have to follow the path I've just come along to the front, so we'd see them.'

'Who has been the leader of this party since I joined it?' inquired Paul coldly.

'You have, and don't we know it!' retorted Fred.

'Apparently you are forgetting what you know,' said Paul. 'If it had not been necessary to have the back door watched, you would not have been sent to watch it.'

'Don't quarrel, for God's sake!' interposed Helen nervily. 'You must forgive him, Paul, if he is a little bored—he hasn't killed anyone for over half an hour.'

'I may soon give him an opportunity to end the boredom,' replied Paul, and turned again to Fred. 'You will be ready then, if necessary, to earn a fourth hanging?'

Fred snapped, 'I've told you before, Your Imperial What-Not, that if there's going to be any hanging, we shall all hang together.'

'In that case—if I interpret your idiom correctly—we must hang together to prevent the catastrophe.'

'Yes, yes, get back!' exclaimed Helen, with a warning glance. 'There can't be two leaders!'

'There speaks wisdom,' added Paul. 'But you need not go back. Stay where you are, if you are certain there is no other way round from the back?'

'There's another way down, but not round,' said Fred. 'The other way ends in a precipice.'

'You have discovered that?'

'By nearly ending there myself.'

'That is satisfactory. Then remain in your present spot, for then you can watch the front of the house too. Fortunately the mist is not quite so thick—'

'What's the idea?' interrupted Fred. 'Aren't you watching the front of the house?'

'He will never be satisfied,' sighed Paul. 'He will even complain to the hangman that the rope is too tight. No, we are not going to watch the front of the house. We are going to watch the inside of the house . . . No, Helen, I am *not* content with your judgment—our judgment, if you prefer it—of Mr Lynch. The mist may breed fancies, but I have a feeling—what is that more expressive word I heard you use once—?'

'Hunch?'

'Ah, hunch. Yes. I have a hunch that things are not progressing too smoothly in there—that we have waited too long—and that it is time for us to discover things for ourselves. Because—and this I may impress again upon you both—there is no—future?—for either of you, or for myself— if we do not complete without any shadow of doubt what we have journeyed here to complete. We needed such a man as Mr Lynch to direct us to the spot. It may transpire that this direction will end Mr Lynch's service to us. You agree?'

'I'm not particularly anxious to go in that house a second time, if that's what you mean,' answered Helen. 'Once was enough.'

'You went alone. Ill prepared. And the odds then were two to one against you.'

'What are the odds now?'

'Excluding the boy, four to one—in our favour.'

'I thought you were doubtful of Lynch?'

'Of his competence . . . You mean?' He paused. 'In that case, it would be three to two. But, even so, the odds would be in our favour, both in number and in brain, and I think, under my direction—and by curbing undue haste and hot-headedness'—he turned to Fred for an instant—'we should be more than a match for a doddering old man and Mr Lynch.'

Then the front door opened, and, outlined against a dim background of candlelight, Mr Lynch beckoned to them.

24

Dead Men's Ears

Standing at the open door, Ben watched two figures change from two-dimensional shadows into three-dimensional solidarity as they approached the porch in response to his beckoning. One figure he knew. The other he could merely identify by his own nickname of the Jack of Clubs; and that was merely a guess, although a correct one.

'Now, don't fergit,' he reminded himself at this moment of crisis. 'You're Joe Lynch. You don't care abart nobody. You've jest bin the blinkinest blackguard anybody could be, and you 'aven't got no 'eart, it's a bit o' stone.'

He did his best to justify this conception while Helen Warren and Paul regarded him.

'Well?' said Paul, for Ben did not move out of the way, but stood blocking the entrance.

''Oo are you?' replied Ben. 'And don't tork so loud!'

The admonition was unnecessary, for Paul's voice had been low, but Joe Lynch had to show that he was up to his job and not afraid of anybody.

'He is your chief,' said Helen quickly. 'You needn't worry about his name.'

'I see—you're standin' fer 'im?'

'Would I be with him if I were not, you idiot!' she retorted.

'I ain't an idiot, and keep yer voice dahn,' replied Ben. 'You engiged a careful man when yer engiged Joe Lynch. Are you two the lot, or is there any more of yer?'

'What does that matter?'

'I'll tell yer. I've done with workin' any more in the dark. It's that's wot near ruined it. 'Ow I've got through to 'ere with all this guessin' and pertendin' beats me, and that's a fack. Is there anybody else outside?'

Helen glanced at Paul, then answered:

'Fred is outside.'

'Wot abart Perjarmer Percy? You know 'oo I mean—that Mr Suttercliff.'

'He is not here,' snapped Helen, 'and mend your manners!'

'Yer didn't engige me fer me manners, so we'll fergit 'em,' returned Ben. 'Git Fred in 'ere.'

'Mr Lynch is quite interesting,' observed Paul, now interposing. 'I will continue the conversation. Why do you require Fred's presence, Mr Lynch, as well as ours?'

'I'll tell yer that when 'e's 'ere.'

'You will tell us now.'

'Wot, will I? Orl right. There carn't be too many witnesses, that's why.'

'Witnesses of what?'

'That's wot I'm goin' ter tell yer when 'e's 'ere.'

'This is your first experience of Mr Lynch,' remarked

191

Helen, with a faint smile. 'I ought to have warned you, Paul.'

'You warned me he was unusual—that I do not mind,' answered Paul. 'If he were also disobedient it would be another matter. Mr Lynch, there is no need for Fred's presence here yet. If the need arises later, I will decide. Is that clear?'

'Well, it's clearer than the weather,' admitted Ben. ''Ave you bin follerin' me orl along the line? Right from the word Go?'

'We have.'

'Didn't trust me, eh?'

'We had to make sure that you completed your work.'

'Well, that's wot I've brort yer in for! No meetin' at the gate, thank yer—when p'r'aps yer mightn't be there, or might give me a push like. If you ain't trusted Lynch, then p'r'aps 'e ain't trustin' you. See, 'e means ter 'ave 'is fifty quid afore 'e leaves this 'ouse—and yer carn't put 'im orf with flash notes!'

Helen gave a little exclamation of exasperation.

'You shall have your fifty pounds, and the notes will be as real as the other notes you've had!' she said. 'But if you delay any longer, you won't get a penny!'

'We'd see abart that!' muttered Ben. 'Orl right. Let's git on with it. Walk inter the parler, as the spider sed ter the fly.'

They stepped in, watchfully. Ben closed the door behind them, and then crossed to the small table on which still lay the box of chocolates. Only now it was open, and some of the chocolates were missing.

'Nice things, chocklits,' he remarked, taking up the box. ''Ave one?'

He turned with the box in his hands. He noticed that both Paul and Helen had produced revolvers.

'Corse, you're barmy!' he said scornfully. 'Do yer s'pose I'd be runnin' abart loose if yer needed them things?'

'You mentioned a moment or two ago that you were a careful man, Mr Lynch,' replied Paul. 'We are merely acting with the same care. Bring the box to us.'

'That's wot I'm goin' ter do.'

He took the box to them. They regarded the contents, Paul calmly, Helen with visible distaste.

'Those big 'uns with the vi'lets on their nobs arc good,' advised Ben. 'Or if yer like corfee creams, those in the corner—'

'For God's sake, stop that!' exclaimed Helen.

'Wot's the trouble?' inquired Ben, suddenly fixing her with his eyes. 'No one's comin'!'

A silence followed his words. Helen glanced towards the door at the back, then raised her eyes to the ceiling.

'Don't 'ear nobody, do yer?' asked Ben.

'There are six chocolates gone,' said Paul.

'Yus, orl gorn,' nodded Ben. 'Three each.'

'What!' exclaimed Helen. She seemed to be having difficulty with her voice. 'Do you mean—'

'That's right,' Ben nodded again. 'Old 'uns like sweets, sime as young 'uns. There's a packet on the table over there. Yer can 'ave it back—it won't be wanted now.'

One of the four candles spluttered. The sound made Helen jump. Ben enjoyed the moment. He wondered how many more moments, enjoyable or otherwise, remained for him.

'Where are they?' asked Paul.

'Up aloft,' answered Ben.

'Then, if we go up, we need not fear them?'

'Well, that derpends on 'ow yer mide. See, there's more'n one kind o' fear.'

He looked at Helen. Through Joe Lynch he was doing his best to pile on the agony, and he did not feel a grain of sympathy as he watched her fighting her nerves. In the warmth and comfort of a luxurious bed she had plotted for the tragedy that was supposed to have occurred in the room above them. In the warmth and comfort of that bed she would have heard of the tragedy's occurrence without turning a hair—probably manicuring her nails the while. Yes, it was right that she should have come to the spot, where she could ironically sense the atmosphere of the tragedy that had not happened!

'No kind of fear troubles *you*?' she inquired, with an undercurrent of defiance.

'Lumme, no!' scoffed Ben. 'I seen a person 'anged once. Fer wot they calls comperlicity. You know, one bloke does it, but the other bloke tells 'im to.'

'I think we do not need any of your memories, Mr Lynch,' suggested Paul. 'But tell me this. If, as you say, we have no need to fear anybody—'

'Well, where's anybody?'

'As you say, where is anybody? And why, therefore, did you warn us to keep our voices low?'

'Oh, I see wot yer mean. But don't *you* always git a feelin' that corpses is listenin'?'

Helen drew a sharp breath.

'Get this over, Paul!' she said. 'There's a limit, you know!'

'Go on!' exclaimed Ben. 'Yer ain't *really* worryin'?'

Paul made a sign with his revolver towards the door.

'Show us the way,' he ordered, 'and waste no more time.'

'Right,' answered Ben, and moved to the table. A quick word from Paul stopped him. 'Wot's up?' he asked.

'Keep that box of chocolates,' replied Paul.

'Why? We've no more use for 'em!'

'Yes, I have another use for them. While you are holding that box—with both hands, please—you cannot hold anything else.'

'Oh, I see! I'm s'posed to 'ave a gun on me!'

'Just a continuation of that carefulness we all believe in, Mr Lynch. Walk ahead. We shall follow.'

'Seems to me yer spends yer life follerin'!' grumbled Ben. 'Never mind, yer'll go fust at the funeral.'

'I shall stay here, Paul,' said Helen. 'Your eyes will be enough. And I couldn't identify him, anyway.'

'As you like.'

'I do like!' As he looked at her rather doubtfully, she added, 'I shan't move from this spot—I'll be here when you come down again.'

'I 'ope she *don't* move from the spot,' thought Ben, as he led the way to the hall. 'That's a noosense!'

Things were not going too well. He had planned that all three should accompany him upstairs, so that the lower floor and the grounds should be clear of the enemy for a short while. Instead, Fred was somewhere outside, Helen was in the sitting-room, and only the tall Jack of Clubs was following him up the staircase to the climax of this episode. What the climax was going to be Ben had no notion. He had planned for the old man and the boy, and was trusting to luck for himself.

Other thoughts raced through his mind as he mounted the stairs, pressing upon him with a kind of hopeless weight. There was MacTavish. If MacTavish had indeed shared the fate of Mr Smith of Boston and the detective on the bridge, he made another reason why the enemy should not merely be thwarted in their present design, but should be captured for the designs they had already put into execution. On Ben alone rested that responsibility to justice and the law. And there was Jean. What about her? With MacTavish gone, she would be alone . . .

Six steps from the top Ben slipped deliberately. He had to do something to gain a few more seconds. His mind was wandering from the moment, and it was the moment on which all the rest depended. He had to find a solution of the situation that would face him when the bedroom door was opened. 'Now, then, think o' somethink!' he urged himself while he slipped. 'Door opens—in we go—and then—think o' somethink!'

'If corpses can hear, they will hear that,' said a low voice behind him.

Yes, and so would the woman waiting in the room below! Suppose his tripping brought her out into the hall, and she got a glimpse of the backdoor . . . Idiot, he was!

'It's these durned sweets,' he mumbled, picking up the box. 'If yer carn't swing yer arms yer loses yer balance. That's 'ow maids drops trays.'

'Well, get your balance again.'

'I'm gettin' it. The things I've bin through, it's a wunner I ain't lorst it orl together!'

They reached the top. Ben strained his ears to hear sounds from the bottom, but he heard nothing. He paused again.

'These nerves, Mr Lynch—are they affecting you, also?'

'Got to git yer breath, ain't yer?' retorted Ben.

'One flight of stairs should not make one lose it. I still have mine.'

'That's a good thing, because you'll want it in 'arf a mo'.'

'You underestimate me. The sight of death affects me as little as, I understand, it affects you. I have probably had even more experience.'

'Go on!'

'Have you ever fought in a battle?'

'Yus, but I always shut me eyes.'

'The English sense of humour, I am often remarking, is a thing beyond my comprehension, but there is something about yours, Mr Lynch, that at times is almost comprehensible. Are you really and truly as—bloodthirsty as you declare?'

'Wot, bloodthirsty?' exclaimed Ben. 'You orter see me workin'!'

'I hope to, one day, but at the moment we are on our way—and not hurrying about it—to see the results of your work. I myself am *quite* as bloodthirsty as I doubtless seem to you. I may make less noise about it, and I do not kill for the mere pleasure of it. But when an object has to be achieved, individual life is a small matter. If I bore you, it is not my fault. I am filling in the time while you are waiting. I do *not* shut my eyes on the battlefield—and I have been on many more than one. Which room is it?'

'Eh? Oh—that 'un.'

'On the left.'

'Yus.'

'I shall regard the two casualties with my eyes well open. And, by the way, I shall not share in any regret that the number is two instead of one. The second might have lived

197

to tell a tale. Now—though you suggest he may be listening—at least, he cannot talk. So why should this not be a murder and a suicide?'

'Eh?'

'The boy was murdered, and his murderer then took his own life by the same means. No—a moment!'

Ben had started to move towards the door.

"Oo's stopping now?' he demanded.

'I am, Mr Lynch. To mention another theory. *Two* murders and a suicide. Mr MacTavish, to whom money was owed by this house, and who hoped to get paid, with a surplus, out of the proceeds of ten thousand pounds, came here for a settlement. He committed suicide, in terror or remorse, after he left. Or perhaps that was just an unfortunate accident in the mist. His legs might conceivably have been unsteady, for—again, why not?— he already had another murder on his conscience. That of Mr Smith of Boston. I admit MacTavish chooses a somewhat curious method of revenge here, and all his motives may not be obvious if we eliminate insanity. But those are little details the English police may like to play with, while we are—elsewhere. To quote your favourite expression—"eh?" Well, we will waste no more time. I require that interesting door on the left open in five short seconds.'

'Yer carn't mike a second shorter'n wot it is,' answered Ben. His own preference would have been to increase the length. 'Leastwise, not in this country.'

He stopped outside the door, removed one hand from the chocolate-box, and began fumbling for the key.

'Really, you are *extremely* careful,' remarked his companion. 'You even lock dead people in rooms!'

'I've known 'em pop out agine afore now,' answered Ben. 'I once saw a chicken runnin' abart without no 'ead.'

'But these are not chickens?'

'That's right. I was jest givin' yer a simultude or wotever they calls it.'

'The key seems—what is the word?—bashful.'

'Eh?'

'You are sure you have it?'

'Yus. It's got stuck ter a bit o' torfee, and I've on'y got one 'and becos' I'm ter 'ang on ter the chocklits. It's your fault if we're losin' time now.'

'Shall I help you?'

'No. It's comin'.'

'Without, let us hope, the toffee?'

Ben did not reply, for at this instant the key came. It came depressingly alone. Not even the fraction of an idea with it.

He inserted it in the lock. He turned it, opened the door an inch, and paused.

'Now fer it!' he whispered.

He shoved the door wide.

'My Gawd!' he shrieked, bounding back.

His companion gripped his revolver firmly and took a step forward. A chocolate-box came hurtling at the back of his head. As he swayed round, a fist struck him, and the door was slammed against his face.

'Now you've lorst *your* balance!' bawled Ben deliriously through the door.

He relocked the door, and the next moment was helter-skeltering down the stairs.

25

Down the Mountain

With the sound of shouting and banging in his ears, Ben reached the bottom of the staircase. There he found his progress barred by Helen Warren's revolver.

'What's happening?' she cried.

'Gawd knows!' gasped Ben. 'They've got 'im!'

'Then why have you come down?'

'Why don't you go up? I ain't got a gun!'

He made a grab, but she drew her hand away swiftly.

'There yer are!' panted Ben. 'It's the gun's wanted up there, it don't matter 'oo uses it!'

The banging continued. The shouting grew louder. At the moment it was incoherent, but if she heard the words . . .

'Gimme the gun and I'll go back! If yer don't, I'm orf!'

He grabbed a second time, but again she was too quick for him. As she sprang back, he suddenly swerved aside and darted towards the backdoor.

The backdoor was ajar. He slammed it behind him. He could not say whether the slam covered a pistol shot or not, but he had a nasty impression that he had only just escaped a bullet.

Outside he stood still for a moment. Partly to collect his wits, and partly because he was confused by the enveloping white mist. Had he been told to turn to the left or the right? He could not remember, it seemed so long ago! In a sudden panic he turned to the left, and just saved himself from leaping down a precipice. He saved himself by sitting down in the air and trying to swim backwards. His hands grabbed ground behind him, and pulled the rest of his suspended frame back through them. It was a feat that could only have been accomplished by a man who had spent most of his life wriggling out of difficulties. Wondering whether he were going to be sick, and convinced that he was, he clambered to his shaking legs, tottered round, and lurched in the opposite direction.

He groped his way round an angle of the house. He ran, with startling abruptness, into a knot of shadowy people. He joined the knot, to find himself entangled in a portion resembling Fred. For an instant he became a separate knot all by himself, and he imagined he was about to experience a new form of death by intensive tying. The prospect was so unpleasant that all at once the knot burst, and the shadowy figures sprayed in all directions, as though a bomb had exploded beneath them. Then he discovered that he was running. He did not remember starting, but he supposed he must have started, or he wouldn't still be doing it. Ahead of him were the faint, constantly dissolving and reappearing forms of an old man and a small boy. Was Fred behind him?

He did not stop to inquire. He caught up the old man and the boy at the gate. Now they were all three outside the gate.

'Why ain't I bein' sick?' wondered Ben. 'I can't mike it out!'

Ahead stretched the beginning of the long, tortuous track to Muirgissie, more than a thousand feet below. They could only see a yard or two of the track. The journey seemed a sheer impossibility. Even if they could reach MacTavish's car before their pursuers overtook them with bullets, how would they be able to turn and drive it?

'Right turn, men!'

The order came in a sudden juvenile whisper. Obeying automatically, Ben blundered into the boy. The boy's face was flushed, and its contrast to the whiteness of the mist made Ben think of robins in the snow on Christmas cards. He thought of ridiculous things at ridiculous moments. Once when he had been nearly drowning he had thought of tomato soup, and the sudden agony of the prospect of never having any more tomato soup had given him the strength that had saved him. Now the boy's flushed face brought him out of the frenzied mental numbness through which his undirected limbs had functioned, and gave him back a little of his lost sense. He forgot his own skin, and thought of the boy's. And also of the old man's, which at this moment was so much whiter.

'I mustn't be sick,' he decided. 'That'd 'old us up!' And while making this heroic decision he managed to murmur, 'Wot's the idea?'

'We can get down to the loch,' whispered the boy, 'only we must be careful.'

'Yes, yes—the boat!' added the old man.

Lumme! Loch! Boat! That *was* an idea! How far down was the boat? Better not inquire, perhaps, in case the figure made one dizzy!

'Can we do it?' Ben asked the old man.

The old man hesitated. His fingers were nervously clutching his revolver. Somehow he had managed to retain that, and suddenly Ben wondered whether the shot he believed he had heard had come from Mr Hymat's revolver, and not from Helen Warren's.

Fresh sounds from the house ended their hesitation. The track to Muirgissie held no hope for them. A precipitous climb—might!

'Step where I step,' came the boy's next order, 'and you'll be all right. I know the way. Very slow march!'

It had to be a very slow march or a disastrously quick one, and in spite of the urgency for speed the order for slow motion was necessary. But the slowness of the motion as they began the descent—the boy leading, the old man next, and Ben last—was agonising while those sounds from the house grew closer and closer. 'If my 'ead ain't below the edge afore they're through the gite,' reflected Ben, 'it'll be popped orf!' The trouble was that it was no good stooping, for when you stooped the ground rose up and hit the part you stooped with, making you sit down and slide. 'Yus, and when Father slides, we orl slide!'

Something clicked above him. The gate? The boy heard it, too, and stopped. Now the sounds seemed immediately overhead.

Ben found himself staring at a large loose stone. In another moment his boot would have kicked it, and it would have descended into the bottomless white pit with a clatter. Even without the impetus of Ben's boot it looked disturbingly insecure. It would go if you breathed upon it. Therefore you didn't breathe.

Now low voices drifted towards them, as though spoken

from the other side of a curtain. The speakers had stopped, like those they were seeking. Out of the incoherent murmuring came two clear words: 'Down there!' Ben swallowed and missed.

The old man was galvanised into action by the words. He turned, raising his revolver. Ben shot out his hand and seized the weapon from him. The action shifted the large stone, and it vanished into the void.

Once more they stood stock still. The picture had leapt into momentary action and was now static again, though something unseen was not static. A stone hurtling through space. The words, 'Down there!' had as yet brought no response, but the response would come when the stone made its next contact with solid matter. Meanwhile, Ben and the old man stared at each other, afraid to shift their eyeballs.

In the agonising seconds that followed the leaping of the stone, and while three heads peered down trying to pierce the white blanket, Ben's grotesquely-fashioned mind recalled the story of the traveller who dropped a boot heavily on the bedroom floor and laid the other boot down gently; the man beneath him, awakened by the first boot, spent the rest of the night expecting the second boot to descend. How long was this stone going to take to descend? Moments such as these always seem like minutes, but surely that illusion could not account for the length of the present waiting? Now for the clatter . . . no? Well, now! . . . No, again? Well, surely, now . . .?

They never heard the stone touch bottom. The ominous silence through a thousand feet of space removed one terror to arouse another. Ben's boot was only a few inches from where the stone had been.

The voices murmured vaguely again. The sounds of steps proceeded, grew fainter, ceased. The menace above them passed on.

But there was no question of returning to the grim house where tragedy had only been averted by a hair's breadth, and where four long candles gave their flickering light to an ominous emptiness. For all the fugitives knew, the house was not empty. Someone might have been left behind. Or, failing that, all three hunters might return when they failed to make their captures along the road. Muirgissie had to be reached and contact established with solid law-abiding people, and the road was so unsafe that even this perilous descent was safer.

'All clear,' muttered Ben, ignoring meteorology.

The old man carried the signal forward, and the journey continued.

Had the descent been actually as steep as it seemed in the mist, or had the boy been less certain of the easiest paths, it is probable that the final tragedy would have been played on this mountainside. The boy's direction was unerring, however, for climbing was second-nature to him and he had descended to the lake by their present route a hundred times. Happily, too, they soon slipped out of the bottom of a thick white cloud, and came upon thinner patches. Now they could see ten yards ahead, not five, and moved in a larger white-walled globe of space.

'Do yer know wot I think, yer Majesty,' said Ben suddenly. They had reached the little plateau, and it was no longer necessary to proceed in single file, though they still had to walk warily. 'I think we're goin' ter win this 'ere little gime!'

Konrad smiled faintly. Apart from his directions, he had not said a word during the whole journey.

'Corse, we ain't quite won yet,' Ben went on. 'We got ter git ter the bottom, ain't we, and then there's that boat. But—well, you're a proper King—see, the Enemy played the gime a bit rougher like than wot they was told, but it didn't worry *you*—and so I thort I'd let yer know I'm proud to serve under yer. And, don't fergit, I've served under Wellington and Nelson and Charles the Fust.'

'Thank you, Royal spy,' answered Konrad.

The words were brave enough, but the voice was not very steady.

'Not a bit,' replied Ben. 'I b'leeve in a spot o' torkin' arter a spot of excitement—it's good fer yer. Me, sime as you. If we go thinkin' too much, lumme, p'r'aps we'd fergit it *is* a gime?'

The boy turned his head, and repeated, as though he were saying a lesson:

'It is a game.'

'That's right. And we're orl playin' it tergether. Come ter that, I sometimes think the 'ole of life's a gime—well, if yer know wot I mean. I've 'ad some funny 'uns! Shipwrecks, trine accidents, cannerbal islands—fack—'aunted 'ouses, dozens o' them—but 'ere I am, ain't I? Jest 'ang on, and yer'll always come through some'ow.'

He tripped as he spoke and fell on his nose.

'See, orl a part of it,' he said, picking himself up.

'I hope I shall understand you one day, Mr Wilkins,' remarked Mr Hymat.

'It don't often 'appen,' replied Ben, 'though, mind yer, it's bin done.'

'I understand you,' said the boy.

'Go on!' exclaimed Ben.

'Yes. And—' He grew a little red, his spirit rebelling

against any outward sign of emotion. 'And you must have a big reward.'

'Not money, yer Majesty,' answered Ben. 'See, we ain't playin' the gime fer that. Jest glory. But I'll tell yer wot I wouldn't mind—bein' mide a knight or somethink—'

They had reached the end of the plateau, and were falling into single file again for their next descent when the boy suddenly stepped back.

'Wot's up?' asked Ben sharply.

He slipped forward and took Konrad's place. A strange sight greeted his eyes. Far below, through the thinning white vapour, was the lake. It glowed with the unexpected illumination of escaping sunlight, looking almost unnatural in its perfect clarity. But it was not the lake that arrested Ben's attention, and that had caused the boy to retreat.

It was MacTavish.

26

Back to Muirgissie

MacTavish lay on his face, a few feet down the slope. He was perfectly still, with one arm stretched out, the other crunched under him. In a slip and a tumble Ben had reached his side.

'Is he—dead?' came Mr Hymat's whisper, as he and the boy crept more cautiously over the edge.

Ben's hand was groping for information. It rested over MacTavish's heart.

'No, 'e ain't dead,' he answered, 'but I'm afraid it ain't a gime no longer.'

'It never was,' said the boy.

'Corse it wasn't,' agreed Ben, 'on'y we kep' it up as long as we could.'

He turned back to MacTavish, and completed his examination. He was no doctor, but he had seen men in every kind of condition, and he had instinct for the signs. MacTavish's signs were pretty bad.

'How did he—how did he fall all this distance?' muttered Mr Hymat.

''E didn't,' replied Ben. ''E fell the fust bit—we know 'oo mide 'im—and 'e crawled the larst. This is where 'e give out.'

'Yes, I suppose so.'

'Yer can see with 'arf a wink.'

'Can we—leave him here?'

'Wot! When 'e ain't dead?'

'We must take him with us,' decided Konrad, 'and we must find a doctor.'

Ben looked at him approvingly. Queer little fellow, this. Reg'ler kid.

'That's the stuff, yer Majesty,' he smiled. 'Yer carn't leave no cashelties on the battlefield—'speshully,' he added, now glancing at the old man, 'when they've worked with yer.'

'Yes, yes, exactly!' frowned Mr Hymat. 'But how are we going to get him down?'

'Gawd knows,' returned Ben. 'Orl *I* knows is that we've gotter.'

Then the boy came out with another suggestion.

'We need a stretcher,' he said.

'Where's the stretcher?' inquired Ben.

'There's a loose seat in the boat.'

'Lumme—you're the goods orl right! We'll git it.'

The question arose, who should get it? Ben quickly vetoed Konrad's suggestion that he should descend alone.

'Why not? It would be quickest,' said the boy, his practical mind working.

'Fust, 'it 'd be 'eavy to bring up alone,' answered Ben. 'Nex', yer mightn't come back agine!'

'I would!'

'Corse yer would, but yer mightn't.'

'We'd better all go down,' suggested Mr Hymat.

209

But Ben again vetoed that obvious suggestion.

'See, we gotter perserve our strength,' he pointed out, 'and we'll need it on the nex' trip!'

Mr Hymat nodded. His strength seemed already spent. He sat down weakly, and stared at the distant water.

''Ow abart this?' said Ben, producing the only alternative that remained. 'I carn't go alone, becos' not knowin' the best way, *I* mightn't come back agine, but if 'is Majesty and me goes tergether, then we'll be sure to come back, on'y would you mind waitin' 'ere by yerself? It ain't, well, cheerful like. 'Corse, you must 'ave yer gun back, so's if you sees anybody not nice you can put a round 'ole in 'em.'

The old man roused himself as Ben held out the revolver.

'No, you keep that,' he said. 'You may need it more than I will.'

'P'r'aps yer right,' agreed Ben. 'Funny 'ow things chinge, ain't it? When I fust called, yer was 'oldin' me up with this 'ere little gun!'

The water was still an unkind distance away, and it took Ben and his guide nearly an hour to reach it, although the last forty yards Ben managed in a split second. After the loose seat had been secured—for the boat, despite fears, was blessedly present, moored to a post—the return journey took them over an hour. It was well past lunch time when Mr Hymat was rejoined. But no one mentioned lunch. Either they had forgotten hunger, or were so conscious of it that they feared to refer to it.

'Any trouble while we was gorn?' asked Ben.

'Nothing,' answered Mr Hymat.

'Wot abart—'as 'e moved?'

Mr Hymat shook his head. Ben examined MacTavish again. The heart was still beating.

'I don't know how we're going to manage it,' muttered Mr Hymat.

'As fur as I can work it out,' replied Ben, 'if yer stop ter think, yer carn't manage nothink, but if yer jest goes on some'ow, it gits done. Do yer s'pose if I'd stopped ter think I'd 'ave come up ter Scotland? Lumme, no! But I'm 'ere, ain't I, and we ain't dead, are we? And MacTavish ain't dead. So let's git 'im on the stretcher, and then see wot 'appens.'

In this spirit they continued with their work, and in this spirit they brought MacTavish down the mountain; taking turns, changing shifts, sometimes carrying the improvised stretcher, sometimes sliding it, many times resting through sheer exhaustion. Mr Hymat had wondered how they were going to manage it. When they had managed it, they still could not have explained how. At the edge of the loch they stared back at the mountain down which they had come with their grim, roped burden. 'Go on!' thought Ben. Yet here MacTavish was, lying in the bottom of the boat, and his heart was still beating.

Thought had remained still during the greater part of that strenuous, hazardous journey. Each new obstacle had been overcome by refusing doggedly to dwell upon it. But occasionally while they rested, the bursting mind behind Ben's perspiring forehead had reverted to other moves in this queer game, and he had wondered how those other moves were progressing. Where were the 'Enemy' at this moment? Had they reached Muirgissie? Were they waiting there, or travelling on beyond? Had they returned to the house of the four candles? . . . Funny, how he kept on thinking of those four candles! They had nothing to do with the case, yet they stuck in his mind, illuminating a constantly-recurring vision of the lonely room with its small toy battlefield invaded by poisoned sweets . . . And what was happening at the Black Swan? Had Jean grown anxious yet, or was she waiting unconcernedly for her uncle's return? And the police—what were they doing? And Mr Sutcliffe—what was he doing? Waiting, also? For the return of Helen Warren? While manicuring his nails?

Well, all these questions, saving perhaps the last, would soon be answered, and meanwhile a boat had to be rowed across a loch.

Mist still swathed the mountain-tops surrounding the loch, but the water itself was clear in the afternoon sunlight that slanted through the lower hills towards Muirgissie. It was, in fact, a perfect afternoon for a boating expedition if moods had been in tune. Ben took the oars. One of his few qualifications, relic of his Merchant Service days, was that he could row.

It was a silent journey, with a queer, uneasy peace as its background. No one knew what lay ahead. That knowledge was happily spared them. But, for a short while, plans did not have to be formed or decisions made, while the procedure once they reached Muirgissie was simply and obviously expressed in two words: Doctor—Police.

Meanwhile, there was nothing to do but to keep the boat going.

Once Ben caught the boy's expression as he stared at the innkeeper's prone figure.

''E ain't dead,' Ben reminded him.

'No,' answered Konrad.

He had fallen into the habit of accepting everything Ben said, whether he really believed it or not.

''E's jest got wot they calls concunshun,' said Ben. 'Yer

gits it at football when yer 'ead 'its the goalpost instead o' the ball. I've 'ad it dozens o' times.'

'How long is it before you wake up?' asked Konrad.

'That derpends on' ow 'ard yer was 'it,' replied Ben. 'Once I got 'it in July and come to fer Christmas.'

'I mean, *really*,' persisted the boy, refusing this time to smile.

Perhaps he was right. Ben often made jokes at the wrong time. But when the time was wrong, it was hard to know.

'Yer can be subconshus fer days, and that's a fack,' he answered solemnly. 'I knew a feller once wot never moved fer three. I give 'im the knock, so I counted. When 'e come to, 'e give me a knock. Mr MacTavish'll be orl right, yer Majesty, once we git 'im to a doctor.'

Presently, while hugging the left shore, they came round a bend, and Muirgissie grew with startling suddenness. A stone wall now ran along the water's edge, with a road beyond, and about fifty yards ahead was a squat projection that was obviously the landing-spot. A low building was by the landing-stage, and Ben twisted his head round to scan it.

'Don't see nobody,' he reported.

'No, it's empty,' answered Mr Hymat. 'That's just as well.'

'Yus, we don't want no recepshun,' said Ben.

A minute later he had shipped his oars, reached the landing-stage, and jumped ashore.

Figures slipped from the low building.

'That is your man,' said a familiar voice. 'Mind his gun.'

Two constables shot forward. Ben found himself in handcuffs.

27

While the Moments Ticked by

What happened next was a series of brilliant, darting stars followed by a black blank. When Ben came out of the blank he was in a small, white-washed room, and a stranger was sitting opposite him. By the stranger was one of the constables who had produced the stars. He had had a few himself, by the look of him.

'Comin' to,' reported the constable.

'Ah,' nodded the stranger, and waited a few seconds till Ben came to a little more.

Ben glanced muzzily at his wrists. They were still handcuffed.

'If you want them off, you'll have to behave,' said the stranger.

'Where's the boy?' muttered Ben.

'Yes, we'll talk about that, when you're ready.'

'Where is 'e, where is 'e?' shouted Ben, jumping up.

The constable pushed him down again. He went down quite easily. The stranger frowned.

'That sort of thing won't help,' he said severely. 'If you

want any questions answered you must behave quietly—
and answer some yourself.'

'Where is 'e?' whispered Ben.

'Safer than he was with you,' answered the stranger.

'Sifer'n 'e was—wot? But I was sivin' 'im!'

The two others exchanged glances.

'Wot d'yer mean? Me 'ead's goin' rahnd. Wot d'yer
mean?'

'I mean,' came the reply, 'that the boy is now safe with
his parents—'

'WOT?'

He jumped up again. Again he was shoved down, this
time less gently.

'Look here, if you can't stay quiet, I'll leave you and
we'll resume our conversation later. Perhaps your head
won't be going round quite so violently in an hour's time!'

'I'll be quiet,' muttered Ben. 'See, me 'ead's stopped.
On'y—that boy—'oo's with him now? That's wot I wanter
know!'

'And that is what I have told you. His parents.'

'They ain't 'is parents!'

'No? Well, we won't worry about them for the moment,
it's you we've got to talk about—'

'But I tell yer, they ain't, they ain't! Lumme, are you a
detective?'

'Yes—'

'Then go orf and cop 'em quick, afore they do the boy
in! It's them wot wants the bricelets, not me! 'Ow long
'ave I bin like this? Where's the old feller—Mr 'Imat—ain't
'e told yer?'

'Come, come, pull yourself together!' ordered the detective
sharply. 'This isn't helping you!'

215

'And he's a good one to talk of doin' in!' observed the constable. 'I suppose he means sweets!'

The detective frowned, but before he could reprimand the constable for the unsolicited comment, Ben exclaimed:

'Sweets? Wot do you know abart sweets?'

'What do you?' retorted the detective. 'Something, evidently?'

Ben stared.

'Does it help your memory, Wilkins,' the detective went on, 'if I tell you that sweets understood to be poisoned have been found at Mr Hymat's house, where the boy was staying? The information did not come from Mr Hymat, but from the boy's parents. Also, some ransom money—notes—'

'Flash 'uns—'

'Oh, you know that, too?'

'Well, yus! See—'

'Wait a moment. I dare say I see a good deal. Perhaps you took those false notes to Mr Hymat's house yourself?'

'Eh?'

'You need not answer unless you want to.'

'Why not? Well, as a matter o' fack, I did tike 'em, on'y—look 'ere, wot are yer gittin' at?'

'I am getting at the fact that, if Mr Hymat was given those notes, he may not have been pleased when he found they were false. And that you may not have been pleased, either, when Mr Hymat informed you. And that, having failed in your design, the sweets alleged to be poisoned might have been used—if the boy's parents had not arrived in time to put you to flight.'

'Like that, eh?' gulped Ben. He raised his manacled hands

216

and wiped his wet forehead with them. 'So that's wot we did?'

'Did you?'

'Tried ter poison 'im—and then they come—and we'ops it?'

'I put the question?'

'Well, put this 'un! If we was doin' that, why didn't we finish the job when we 'ad the boy on the lake, and pop 'im in? Yus, and the innkeeper, too! Did we kill *'im?*'

'If you made the attempt, it did not succeed. A doctor is with him now.'

'Thank Gawd fer that, any'ow!' The detective raised his eyebrows. 'Oh, corse, I fergot I'm a murderer. But some murderers 'as kind 'earts. Did I murder Smith o' Boston, too?'

'Smith of Boston?' repeated the detective slowly. 'Do you mean the man who was found last night about a mile from here—shot?'

'That's the bloke!'

'Yes, and that's the case that originally brought me here. We circulated his description, but the first theory that he was—not Smith of Boston—was confirmed only a few minutes ago. His name is Wilkins. Like yours. Coincidence, eh?' Suddenly the detective's eyes hardened. 'Wilkins—who has been identified—was engaged to bring those false notes to the Black Swan, from where MacTavish would lead him to the house of the kidnapped boy. The boy's parents were behind Wilkins, and hoped to trace their son by this trick. But somebody killed Wilkins. Somebody took those notes to MacTavish, and forced him to complete the journey to the kidnapper's house. Then somebody tried to kill MacTavish by pushing him down a mountain. The rest,

I've already told you. Now, then, let's have *your* story? Perhaps they'll fit? And who is this Smith of Boston?'

Even Ben's unsubtle mind was able to realise the devilish ingenuity of the manœuvre by which the enemy had turned the tables and safeguarded their skins. Of course there were flaws in their tale, and time would reveal some of them. When MacTavish recovered he would be able to deny that Ben had been his aggressor—provided MacTavish had seen his aggressor. Mr Hymat would be able to disprove the accusation that he was a kidnapper—provided he was not a kidnapper. Someone would come forward and identify the dead man as Mr Smith of Boston—provided he *was* Mr Smith of Boston.

But time was the essential factor. And, with all its flaws, the story was more creditable than the story Ben had to tell. With no living soul to corroborate him, would anyone believe Ben's story, even if he possessed the lucidity and memory to tell it?

While the detective waited for him to speak, a dull despair stole over him. The thought that the boy had been captured, and that the game in which they had both put their faith was lost, made every bone in his body ache, and his heart leave its cavity. He recalled once more, while the horrible, fatal seconds ticked by, the lonely room with the four candles, and now in the torturing vision the candles had nearly burnt themselves down and were flickering and spluttering in their sockets. In a few moments they would go out, and the table on which stood the last game of soldiers would be blotted out by darkness . . .

Konrad! Yes, what about Konrad? Surely *he* had supplied the flaw in the Enemy's story? A boy knows his own parents!

218

'The kid—wot's '*e* say?' challenged Ben suddenly.

'He has not said anything,' answered the detective, rather dryly.

'Why not?'

'If you had been less busy trying to maim the police force, you would know why not. He fainted as his father lifted him out of the boat, and he hadn't come to when they reached the inn.'

'Fainted!'

'Hardly surprising. He's been through a stiff time—'

''E's bin through a stiffer time than you know anything abart!' shouted Ben, leaping up, and this time the constable could not push him down. '*And 'e ain't the kind wot faints!* The inn, eh? Is that where they've took 'im. Git aht o' me way! Git orf me! I'm goin' ter see if 'e's still alive, if you ain't! Orl right—yer've arsked fer it!'

He went into a spin. No one in Muirgissie, or possibly in the whole of Scotland, had ever seen it happen before. As he spun round he extended his clasped hands, and the hand-cuffs revolved into the constable's face. When the constable rose, the prisoner had gone, and the detective also. But the prisoner was leading.

28

Last Lap

Five days previously—five days that seemed like five months—Ben had told the detective on the bridge that the only thing he was really good at was running away. Whether or not he possessed any other qualifications for the queer, uneasy battle of life, this one undoubtedly came first. His experience in fleeing was unrivalled, and was only mitigated by the fact that he did not flee solely in his own cause. Once he had fled a mile to divert a mad dog from an old woman. It was not his fault that the dog belonged to the old woman, and that, after obediently chasing him the mile, it had proved to be saner than Ben.

Now, for the sake of a small boy he had known only a few hours, he performed his *pièce de résistance*. His pace at first was impeded by his handcuffs, since it is difficult to keep your balance at top speed when you cannot swing your arms; but he even made use of this handicap, and just as his pursuer was overtaking him he used his imprisoned wrists to execute another spin—the method was to hurl them round and yield to their weight—and while the detective was spinning round after him he was up a turning.

Then he got into his stride. He was rounding another turning almost before his pursuer had rounded the first. Scurrying footsteps and angry shouts grew more distant. He dived through a padlocked gate, bounced into a low haystack, slid over it, and shot into a shed.

The scurrying footsteps and the angry shouts came closer again, but they passed the gate, and faded out.

Well, that was that. For the moment.

He crept out of the shed and took his bearings. The field was on a slope, and at the bottom was the road that ran beside the loch. Somewhere along that road was the Black Swan.

He crept to the bottom of the hill. Just before emerging on to the road he tried to dispose of his hands, lest they should arouse the curiosity of anyone he met. He could not put them in his pockets, nor could he hide them behind his back, but he managed to fold them inwards against his chest and to obtrude his elbows as though he were dancing the sailor's hornpipe. The only trouble was that, if he actually danced the hornpipe, this would attract more attention than the handcuffs.

Luck was with him on the road. He met no one. This was partly due to the fact that he covered the distance to the inn in less time than it had ever been covered in before. As he reached it a figure emerged.

He stopped abruptly and pressed himself into a wall. The figure—a man in a black coat, carrying a small brown bag—glanced vaguely in his direction, then walked away in the other. An instant later Ben was in the hotel. Two arms caught him. He stared into the face of Jean.

He looked at her stupidly for a moment, while she looked stupidly back. 'Git on with it!' he chided himself. 'Yer ain't doin' nothink!' He felt suddenly weak. He had been running very hard on a very empty stomach, and he was still suffering from bumps.

'You're ill! I'll call the doctor back!'

Jean's voice revived him. Nice to hear it again. Nice to see her friendly unantagonistic eyes. Nice that she seemed concerned about him . . . So that had been the doctor . . .

Her expression changed abruptly. She noticed his hands.

'Where is 'e?' gasped Ben.

But she could not take her eyes off his hands.

'Never mind abart that! Where is 'e? The boy? Where is 'e?'

The vehemence of his questions whipped her into practicality. Sensible girl, Jean . . .

'He'll be all right. The doctor said so. His parents are lookin' after him.'

'Where's the room?'

'He's—he's not to be disturbed—'

'Where's the room? Never mind the bricelets. You know I'm stright, don't yer? Quick! Up ter the room!'

'But we canna—'

'Gawd, do you know wot they're doin'? Murderin' 'im!'

Her eyes dilated. She turned and sped up the stairs. Ben stumbled after her. He saw her open a door without knocking, and he heard a sharp exclamation from inside.

'What's the meaning of this!' cried a familiar voice.

'I'm the meanin' o' this!' bellowed Ben, hurtling past the girl before she could answer.

A scene in which there had been movement suddenly became static, saving for the new character who had abruptly shot into it. The boy lay on a bed. The woman was holding up the boy's head. The man was standing by them, with a glass. The next moment the glass was smashed to smithereens.

'So you've escaped?' said Paul, quietly.

'Don't worry, the pleece are arter me,' panted Ben, 'and I'm waitin'—'*ere*!'

'You shall certainly wait here,' answered Paul, after a quick glance at Helen. 'Come—we must report this!'

For once Ben's speed was outmatched. He made a grab, and as he missed something hit him and he toppled to the ground. Then the ground hit him. Then he heard lightning footsteps, and a door close, and a key turn; and then he heard himself laughing. He couldn't make out at first why he was laughing. All at once he discovered.

'This is why,' he explained to Jean's face, through a thickening haze. 'Lovin' parents 'ave left their kid with a murderer. 'Ow's that fer a joke? Where are yer? Oi! Yer'd better git 'old o' me somewhere—I b'leeve I'm gittin' concunshun.'

29

Sir Ben

For two days, in a pleasant bedroom of the Black Swan, Ben endured a period of luxurious discomfort.

The discomfort at first was considerable. It involved nightmares, in one of which he was burning in a long candlestick while the dead detective watched him and told him to stick it out. When he had stuck it out, and slipped from the nightmares back to reality, his head ached, his wrists ached, his bones ached, and his bumps ached. 'In fack,' he murmured once to his nurse, Jean, 'the on'y bit o' me that don't ache is me missin' tooth.'

'Dinna talk!' retorted Jean. 'Have I no' told you before?'

That was part of the luxury. He wasn't to talk, and he wasn't to move, and he wasn't to think. He was just to eat things and drink things when they were brought to him, and lie quietly when they were not. 'The way that gal's nursin' me,' he reflected, 'yer'd think I was a bloomin' quad!' It was through her that the luxury exceeded the discomfort, and that Ben's opinion of illness underwent revision. This was enough to make a bloke fall ill on purpose.

The one bump of his many that was not sufficiently attended to was his bump of curiosity. He wanted to know things, but the moment he began asking questions Jean jumped his head off. Ay, everything was all right. Ay, everybody was all right. Dinna *worry*!

'The fairst thing the doctor asks me is, "Are ye keepin' him quiet?" and wha' will I tell him?'

'Is the boy orl right?' inquired Ben.

'If I hae told you aince, it's a dozen!' she retorted. 'He's fine!'

'Well, can I see 'im?'

'Ye canna see naebody!'"

'Wha' aboot your uncle?' grinned Ben, and then stopped grinning because it hurt.

'He's no mendin' so quick as you, but he's mendin', and now will I put the pillow over your mouth?'

After all, since these essentials were satisfactory, why worry over the rest, saving for the fun of drawing her sauce? He would know the lot, he expected, before long.

But one point, which he did not mention, continued to perplex him. He had been arrested, and he had escaped handcuffed. Surely a policeman or two should be popping about? The absence of officialdom in any form was almost uncanny.

But on the evening of the second day, an official called. Ben did not know he was an official when Jean announced his name, for Stephen Gerard might be anybody. 'Sounds like terlerphones,' he thought as Jean disappeared to bring the visitor in. He closed his eyes, and wondered vaguely whether he'd got into some new entanglement with a telephone exchange. Then he opened his eyes, and found Stephen Gerard standing by his bed.

'Lumme!' he muttered, and shut his eyes again quickly. He fought dizziness. Was the concunshon returning? He was in the long candlestick once more, and the dead detective was watching, telling him to stick to it. He opened one eye. The dead detective was still there. He opened the other eye. Even that didn't banish him.

'Go on!' he murmured weakly.

'Take it easy,' said Gerard.

'If yer can find a plice where it don't 'urt,' answered Ben, 'will yer pinch it?'

Gerard smiled.

'Well, Ben, whatever you've been through, it hasn't changed you,' he remarked.

Jean behind his shoulder was also smiling.

'*You've* chinged,' replied Ben, now facing reality more clearly. 'Arm in a sling . . . That's funny! There was somethink wrong with yer arm when I saw yer in the nightmare.'

'What nightmare?'

'One of 'em. One o' the fust. There yer was—'

'Yes, there I was,' interposed Gerard, turning his head for a moment to glance at Jean. 'You were babbling about a long candlestick.'

'Eh? 'Owjer know that?'

'Because I was really there, Ben,' said Gerard. 'I'd just arrived. But I had to go away again almost at once—on some business. And now I'm back.'

'Yus, you're back orl right,' muttered Ben. 'Tork abart resuserterlashun!' He paused. 'Business, eh? P'r'aps I can guess it?'

'Wouldn't surprise me.'

'Did yer catch 'em?'

Gerard turned to Jean again. 'All right for the patient to talk?'

'Just to you, I'm thinkin',' she answered. 'He'll burst if he doesna!'

'You've got an understanding nurse,' said Gerard.

'I'll tell yer somethink,' answered Ben. 'When she's nursin' yer, it's a pleasure ter be ill.'

Jean coloured.

'Well, you'll no be wantin' your nurse the now,' she retorted, 'so I'll leave you.'

'You'll do nothing of the sort,' exclaimed Gerard, definitely. 'You'll sit down. And so will I. I've got a bit of understanding, too, and he needs both of us. I'm not going to be left alone with him if he goes off into any more nightmares!'

'You look as if you've 'ad a few,' returned Ben, as they pulled up chairs. 'Why ain't you dead?'

'Yes, let's begin there. I am not dead because I can get over a bad bump as well as you can. I was shot in the arm, and a crack on the pavement finished me. When I came to—well, you'd gone.' His voice became grave. 'You were carrying on.'

'That's right,' nodded Ben. 'Like I said I would.'

'Did you?'

'Didn't I? Well, any'ow, when I saw yer lyin' there—I thort I would.'

'And then wot 'appened?'

'Are you bein' funny?'

'What do you mean?'

'If yer arsked me wot *didn't* 'appen, I might be able to tell yer! Everythink 'appened, and then some! The bloke wot shot yer come along with a woman and I goes orf with 'em in their car like I was Joe Lynch, see, they thort yer was goin' ter shoot Joe Lynch yerself, the way yer raised yer gun—'

'I did kill Joe Lynch,' interposed Gerard, grimly.

'Eh? Oh, yus, the real 'un!'

'Well, and then?'

'Then we was chiced by the pleece, and I thinks, "Lumme, wot's goin' ter 'appen ter me if we're copped?" See, I thort you was dead, so there wasn't nobody ter speak fer me.'

'You took a big risk, Ben.'

'Yus. Arsk me why, and I couldn't tell yer!'

'I know, without your telling.'

'Go on! Why?'

'Well—you might be a fairly decent chap.'

'I'm thinkin' the same,' murmured Jean. Ben began to feel uncomfortable.

'Corse, I see wot yer mean,' he mumbled, 'on'y—well, it wasn't nothink like that. See—well, if yer want it stright, I knows meself, but sometimes, jest once or twice, things git on top of yer, and yer do things yer never thort yer would, in fack, yer 'ardly know yer done 'em till yer done 'em, if yer git me?'

'I get you,' answered Gerard. 'I get you exactly. And then?'

'Eh? Oh, then we goes to a flat, there was a play once called "The Silent 'Ouse," I know becos' I uster pass it, there was a corfee shop near, p'r'aps yer know it, well this orter've been called "The Silent Flat," tork abart quiet, if yer dropped a pin it banged—'

'Can you tell me where it was?'

'Afraid I carn't. See, I was took there in the dark, and when I left it was dark. There was a 'arf-dotty chap there

228

wot lived in a dressing-gown, but 'e didn't seem to 'ave nothink to do with anythink, I put 'im dahn as one o' them giggliots.'

'Giggliot?'

'You know, them French chaps wot, well, 'ang about,'

'What happened at the flat?'

'Nothink. Jest waitin'. And then one night I was took orf in a car to a plice called Boston—'

'Boston?' exclaimed Gerard.

'Yus.'

'Go on.'

'I was goin' on. And in Boston I was passed on like to a man wot drove me 'ere—'

'Smith?'

'Yer know 'im?'

'Tell you in a minute. Yes?'

'Then you know 'e was killed?' Gerard nodded. 'And 'oo killed 'im?'

'You're telling this story.'

'Yus, and I thort *you* was goin' ter!'

'Mine'll come in a moment. Who killed Mr Smith?'

'Well, I wasn't there. See, I on'y come upon 'im arter they'd done it. I'd left 'im jest afore, when 'e'd give me a card with my next nime on it ter show—'

He stopped abruptly, and looked at Jean.

'To show my uncle,' she finished for him. 'You needna hide what's known a'ready.'

'Well, 'ere's somethink that's gotter be knowd,' said Ben. 'Wotever 'er uncle was up to—and as fur as I can mike out, 'e was on'y, well, tryin' to mike a bit, sime as Mr Smith—*she* didn't know nothink abart it. Lumme, she was near orf 'er 'ead with worry, and if anybody tries to mike it out any dif'rent, then by Gawd there'll be another murder!'

'Jean is as straight as you are, Ben,' replied Gerard, smiling. 'She is not worrying now about anything.'

'How could I, wi' such friends?' added Jean, her eyes suspiciously bright.

'I reckon she knows 'ow to be a friend,' answered Ben. 'If she 'adn't—well, bin like wot she is—that boy'd 'ave bin killed. It was she wot sived 'is life, and don't nobody fergit it! My throat's gittin' dry. Wot abart a spot o' water?'

She jumped up and brought him a glass, while Gerard looked at her thoughtfully. Then he turned back to Ben, and said:

'You were followed to Muirgissie—in fact, right to the end—by the people who killed Mr Smith.'

'That's right,' gulped Ben.

'And who claimed they were following you to protect their son—Konrad—but who actually were not related to him at all.'

'Corse they wasn't!'

'And whom you prevented from killing Konrad by a split second—'

'No, that was 'er.' Ben jerked his head towards Jean. 'Anybody else would 'ave stood in me way. Orl I did was ter knock the glass dahn when I got there.'

'Well—we'll award the medals later . . . And who then bunked down to their car, where the chauffeur was waiting, touched seventy or eighty for half a dozen miles, and then—'

He paused.

'Yus?' asked Ben.

'Escaped by aeroplane.'

Ben stared.

'Yer don't mean—arter orl we done—they got away?' he exclaimed.

'The boy has been saved.'

'That's right.'

'Mr MacTavish has also been saved. His convalescence will be considerably longer than yours, but he will live to be a wiser and a better man.'

'I'll see he does!' nodded Jean.

'Jean is happier than when you first came here. A poisonous organisation that was even poisoning the good mountain air of Muirgissie has been broken up. It doesn't seem to me, Ben, that we have done so badly?'

'So we ain't,' agreed Ben. Then added, 'And *you* didn't do so bad to git on to it! 'Ow did that 'appen?'

'Well, while you were on the heels of two of our party, the police were already interested in the third, who had arrived from the Continent—'

'The Jack o' Clubs!'

'What's that?'

'Eh? Oh, on'y my pet nime fer 'im. Go on.'

'Let's keep it, though I don't see the connection. The Jack of Clubs came from a rather disturbed part of Europe, and he was traced one day in Boston, talking to our friend Smith. Then we lost the Jack of Clubs. Then we lost Smith. And just as I was getting over my little indisposition, a description of Smith was circulated among all stations in an attempt to identify him and find his murderers. Disobeying doctor's orders, I came to Muirgissie at once— but, of course, the birds had flown.'

'You wouldn't 'ave disobeyed doctor's orders, not if you'd 'ad my nurse!' grinned Ben.

'Do you know, I believe I would—even *your* nurse,' answered Gerard, slowly. 'You see, Ben, I had a hunch— from little details—that if I came to Muirgissie and traced your Jack of Clubs, I might also trace *you*. And I'd damn well made up my mind to find you.'

'Well, I'm blowed!' murmured Ben.

'I found you babbling about candlesticks. I cleared you with the local police, and gave instructions that you were not to be bothered. Jean saw that my instructions were carried out, while I chased—unsuccessfully—the people we were after. I believe she kept the local constable off once with a toasting fork! And now I'm back . . . And have brought somebody with me.'

He rose suddenly. 'You look tired, Ben. But do you think you could stand one more visitor tonight, for just three minutes? To—meet the somebody. A rather small boy?'

A funny thing happened to Ben. You couldn't always tell from his remarks just how he was feeling—which is the same, after all, with the rest of us—and he often didn't know himself. He knew now that he was tired, but he did not know why the mention of that rather small boy brought a sort of a lump into his throat. For a moment he wondered whether he could stand those three minutes. But he wasn't going to miss them, even if he couldn't.

'You bet!' he muttered.

A few moments later the small boy came into the room, and the others melted out of it.

'Hallo, Royal Spy,' said the boy.

''Allo, Yer Majesty,' answered Ben.

'I really am a King,' replied the boy.

'Corse yer are,' nodded Ben. 'A proper one.'

'Have they told you, then?'

'They didn't need ter. I got funny bones, and *they* told me. There's one be'ind me left knee tells me anythink if I arsk it.'

The boy bit his lip. Then he stood very straight.

'Someone's come for me,' he said. 'I'm going back.'

'That's why the lump came,' thought Ben. 'See I knew that, too.' Aloud he said, 'Vivy le Roy.'

'Mr Hymat's going with me,' Konrad went on, after a pause. 'He's been very good. You see, my father was killed, and when I got away he was supposed to kill me, too. They paid him a lot of money to. But he didn't. He hid me here, and used the money. Then he—he let them know I wasn't dead, and sent for some more. You see, he hadn't any left, and he'd had to borrow some from Mr MacTavish. I don't quite understand it. But that's how everybody got to know. They tried to kill me again the first time. You see, there is what you call a usurper. But the second time you came, and you saved me, so, well, I must make you that knight.'

He stretched out his hand and put it on Ben's head.

'What's your real name?'

'Ben.'

'It is now, Sir Ben.' He kept his hand there for a second, to press the knighthood well in, and then withdrew it. 'I—I suppose—you couldn't come with us, Sir Ben?'

Sir Ben's heart took a silly leap, and then settled down.

'I wouldn't be no good aht there,' he answered, smiling. 'But I'll tell yer wot. If yer ever in any more dinger, jest let Sir Ben know, and 'e'll pop along.'

The boy bit his lip again. Three minutes was going to be ample for both of them.

'What will you do?' he asked.

233

'Well, I never knows, fer certin,' replied Ben. 'But p'r'aps I'll stay on 'ere fer a bit. You know, 'elp with the pots and pans. See, now you're orl right, there's some 'un else wot might like a 'and. The gal 'ere. Did they tell yer, yer Majesty—it was 'er wot really sived yer life? If she 'adn't bin quick, like she was—well, see, orl I did was jest ter knock—I mean, well never mind. Any'ow, wot abart mikin' 'er Lady Jean?'

'I will,' said Konrad.

Suddenly he held out his hand. They shook. Then he turned on his heel smartly, and marched out of the room.

'I wish I didn't blub so easy,' thought Ben.

THE END